Death on the Norwich Express

A DCI GREG GELDARD NOVELLA

by

Heather Peck

Ormesby Publishing

Published in 2024 by Ormesby Publishing

Ormesby St Margaret

Norfolk

www.ormesbypublishing.co.uk

British Library Cataloguing in Publication Data

A CIP catalogue record for this book is available from the British Library.

Page design and typesetting by Ormesby Publishing

Contents

Ve need to tape off Coach C and the buffet car, for forensics ɔ give them a good going-over.'

By the time Bill was waiting alongside the buffet-car oor, Chris was pleased to see the reassuringly sturdy figure f DCI Greg Geldard hurrying down the platform. She ɔdded to the guard to open just that door and smiled ɔwn at the two faces below.

'Doc's on the way, and Ned's on standby if needed,' said reg. 'Okay, let's take a look.'

'What about the passengers?' asked Chris.

'I'm happy with your arrangements. Dr Paisley will be re in minutes, so let's see what she says, and unless she s any concerns we'll go ahead as you proposed. It won't l them to wait a few minutes more.'

Okay. He's here in Coach C.' Chris led the way as they : Bill and his assistant deploying crime scene tape. The ınecting door sighed open, and Greg approached the n lying in the space between the rows of seats.

ꜱtopping a couple of feet away, he asked, 'You checked signs of life?'

I touched his neck. No carotid pulse. That's when I ed the guard over. He was at the end of the carriage.'

'he body was on its back along the aisle, the feet toward front of the train, arms by its sides.

Vhere was he sitting?'

n one of those single seats, facing the direction of travel.'

)o you know who was in the seat opposite?' Greg asked.

es. Me,' Chris replied. Greg turned sharply.

1

A sudden death

'Hi Chris.' Greg answered on his hands-free, peering over his shoulder as he did so, hoping for the opportunity to pull into the outside lane and overtake the slow lorry full of retired hens in front of him. 'Are you home yet?'

'Am I thump!' she responded. There was a distinctly grumpy tone in her voice. 'I'm managing a crime scene at Norwich station.'

Stepping hard on his accelerator as an opportunity manifested itself, Greg replied, 'Why you? I thought you'd be back in your car and on your way home by now.'

'So did I, but a dead body has put the mockers on that.'

'Where?'

'At the station, as I said, or near enough. I've reported it, and I'm waiting for back-up, so I can't go anywhere yet.'

'Details?' asked Greg, signalling to leave the A47 at the next exit and head back to Norwich.

'Male, IC2, around the mid-thirties at a guess. Smartly dressed, wallet contains credit cards in the name of Brett

Wallace but there's no phone, bag or laptop that I can see. Rapid collapse after drinking railway coffee, but I don't think we can blame the coffee as such, even if you do think it's muck. It could be natural causes, but something doesn't sit right with me. I've cleared the other passengers out of this carriage and asked the train staff to keep everyone on the train until the cavalry arrive. It's making me a bit unpopular,' said Chris, with a masterly grasp of understatement.

As she put her phone back in her bag, a shouting match was in full play at the end of the first-class carriage.

'Let me through at once,' an indignant voice was demanding. 'Don't you know who I am? I have an important meeting and I cannot be held up like this. Whatever has happened here, is nothing to do with me.' The hard-pressed guard turned to Chris with considerable relief.

'This police officer will answer your questions,' he said to the burly man with white hair who was making all the fuss.

'I,' he said with hauteur, 'am Sir Alexander Smythe, Director of NHS England, and I am now late for an important meeting with the Norfolk Clinical Commissioning Group. I demand that you instruct this fellow to release the train door and let me depart forthwith.' Chris was not taken with the hectoring tone and exchanged a feeling glance with the train guard.

'Sorry, can't do that, sir,' she said. 'This is a suspicious death, and until my colleagues arrive to take your names and contact details, no one is going anywhere.'

'Who are you to speak to me like that?' dem irate knight of the realm, eyeing the petite wom green trousers and acid yellow jacket with some

'Detective Sergeant Chris Mathews, Norfolk responded, and turned away as vibrations from signalled yet another message.

Waiting on the platform. The boss will join us the staff the train can now come into the platfor

As she read, the train began to move slowly, interrupted journey into the station.

As it drew to a halt with squealing br spotted the familiar figure of Detective Co Street along with two uniformed colleague remained closed, and Chris took to her phon before I give them the okay to open any do organised, or the Gadarene swine will have no lot on the train. I hope there's a few more of

'Two more at the exit,' said Bill. 'More sta

'Okay. One of you go to the end of the make sure we're ready to get names and c from everyone before they leave the platform staff to open selected doors manually, so all will be exiting from the carriage nearest t no one's going anywhere until Greg or Ji arrangements.

'In the meantime, the guard will open buffet car. Bill, you and the other constab through that door. I'll be there, making s the last three carriages moves through into

'That puts a different complexion on it,' he said. 'Okay, let's get your statement first. What did you see? Hang on, let's record this,' – he produced his phone – 'it'll save time later.'

'I got on the train first and sat in the seat there, with my back to the engine. The seat was reserved for me. He got on later, probably a few minutes later, because I'd already settled in my seat and got my iPad out to do some paperwork. I think we nodded to each other, you know, the way you do, and he sat down. As you see, he didn't take his jacket off, and the only thing he put in front of him on the table was his phone. There was the usual bit of jostling for foot space under the table, then I think the train left soon after.'

'Did you leave your seat during the journey?'

'Yes. I went to the loo, I think between Manningtree and Ipswich. He was okay when I got back. The trolley service came past between Ipswich and Diss. We both had coffee and biscuits.'

'Did he leave his seat?'

'Not as far as I know. Not while I was sitting there anyway.'

'How was the coffee served?'

'Poured from a jug into the paper cups.'

'And the biscuits?'

'We picked ready-packaged biscuits from a tray, held out to us. There're probably crumbs still on the table. Ah, here's the doc.'

Dr Paisley came aboard the train with an inappropriately cheery grin. 'Afternoon, Madame Poirot,' she said.

'Oh ha bloody ha,' responded Chris. 'Liverpool Street to Norwich is no Orient Express, believe me.'

Dr Paisley stepped to one side while photos were taken of the body in situ, then she took a closer look. 'You don't need me to tell you how long he's been dead,' she commented. 'I gather you were around at the time. Were you present when he lost consciousness?'

'Yes,' replied Chris. 'I was just explaining to Greg. We'd both had a coffee served to us. He drank his quite quickly; I was sipping mine. When I looked up I thought he didn't seem well. He was pulling at his collar as though he was having difficulty breathing, and he was very pink in the face. Then he really started to struggle for breath, tried to say something, and his head fell forward onto the table. I got out of my seat as quickly as I could, pressed the button for assistance, then when I saw the guard was just at the end of the carriage, I shouted for help. The guard came rushing toward me, I turned back to the casualty, and I think by then he'd gone. I felt for a pulse at his neck, but there was nothing. The guard and I pulled him into the aisle, and I started CPR while the guard radioed for help.'

Dr Paisley took only moments to confirm death, then stood up again. 'Given that you already know when he died, there's no more I can do here,' she said. 'I need him back at the mortuary for a post-mortem.'

'Nothing for us on cause of death?' asked Greg.

›ty and we'll use the four seats nearest the door
vs. That way there'll be minimum interference
nainder of the carriage.

raised his voice to a shout, making an older
n jump. 'Bill, put someone on the door in your
:d, then you come in here, while Chris and I do
vs.'

tiously repeating 'Excuse me,' Chris made her
ie carriage to the next, carrying out a headcount
, and disappeared briefly. By the time Bill had
she had reappeared at the far end and nodded.

id Greg. 'Who was sitting in Coach C during
' Would you please put your hands up?' Five
up: the young couple, an elderly man with a
ıd another couple sitting opposite each other
immediately guessed to be work colleagues,
shared paperwork and laptops on the table
n.

u,' said Greg. 'We'll see you first,' he said to the
hen you five passengers.'

one minute,' exploded Sir Alexander, rising
indignation. 'I have an important meeting to
I have to take part in this charade, I demand
›riority.'

one die if you're late?' asked Greg.

3ut...'

v more minutes won't matter, will they? We'll
; soon as we can.' Greg shouldered past as
: could manage then turned to the guard.

'Not till I've done the post-mortem. All I can say for the moment is that there's no obvious cause of death in what appears to be a man who is healthy in every respect, except that he's dead. No obvious wounds or injuries, I mean. Nor any obvious signs of disease. All I can suggest is that you carry on treating this as a suspicious death, and I'll get back to you as soon as I can.'

A clatter on the steps into the buffet car announced the arrival of Ned, Greg's much respected crime scene manager, and the rest of his immediate team. 'Good timing,' said Dr Paisley. 'I'll leave him to you and the funeral director.'

2

Asking questions

'Everyone out of here,' said Ned. 'Let's treat this as a crime scene until we know different. Bad enough you lot have been paddling about without anyone else joining in.' He shooed Greg, Chris and the guard toward the rear of the train, then turned to Bill at the door. 'Bill, no one except my team in this coach or the buffet car until I say so.'

Greg and Chris moved obediently to the next coach. As the door sighed open, a middle-aged man with white hair and a rubicund complexion leaped to his feet from a seat near the door.

'At last!' he exclaimed in rich and loud tones. 'Do you know—'

'Yes, I do,' interrupted Chris in a determinedly deadpan voice. 'DCI Geldard, meet Sir Alexander Smythe. He is 'a' director of NHS England,' she added pointedly.

'And I need to get to my meeting,' said Sir Alexander. 'At once!'

'If you'd just take a seat,
to you as soon as we can.' I
he moved into the carriage
everyone here in this carria
passengers in the carriages

'There's only one more
guard behind him, and a
chipped in.

'There's no one in the n
looked over the heads of t
spokesperson at the far en
black, wearing a red cap o

'Thank you,' he said.
There were the usual lov
question, and he went o
we're grateful for your
Inspector Geldard,' – he
this is Detective Sergeant
and the knight of the re
He grunted but remained
know, there has been a
have to treat it as a sus
low murmurs; a young
exchanged glances and
hand in his.

'I'm afraid you mu
have completed prelimi
contact details. Then yc
in an aside, 'pop dowr

sure it's em
for intervie
with the re

'Bill.' H
lady near hi
place, tell N
the intervie

Conscien
way down t
as she did s
joined Greg

'Okay,' s
the journey
hands went
bald head, a
whom Greg
as they had
between the

'Thank yo
guard, 'and

'Now jus
to his feet in
attend and i
you give me

'Will som

'Well, no.

'Then a fe
get to you a
politely as h

'Follow me,' he said, gave Bill a meaningful nod, and joined Chris in the end carriage.

'Take a seat,' he said to the guard. Chris already had a recorder on the table in front of her, and her notebook at the ready. Greg took the seat beside her as the guard sank into the seat opposite with a sigh of relief and removed his cap.

'I'll be glad when today is over,' he remarked. 'How can I help?'

Greg looked at him in silence for a moment, noting the line of suntan that stopped where his uniform cap had sat, the fair hair flecked with white above the ears, and the pale grey eyes. Around fifty years old, he estimated, and pretty fit for his age too. Facing the lean man opposite, he subconsciously sucked in the beginnings of a tummy.

'Your name and address?' he asked.

'Tim Nugent. Twenty-two Hillside, Costessey.'

'How long have you worked as a guard?'

'Since 2000, so over nineteen years now.'

'All with Greater Anglia?'

'Ten with Greater Anglia, and GNER before that.'

'Tell me about today.'

'It was a normal trip. The train was late – that's not unusual – but the one before us was too, so some of the passengers who should have been on this service got the earlier one. That's why it was so quiet. The buffet car was short-staffed – that's not unusual either – so the First Class trolley service was late. The buffet-car attendant, Janice, served the first rush of customers from Standard, then closed the buffet car and nipped round with an abbreviated trolley service in First. Just drinks and biscuits really.'

'Where is she now?' asked Chris. 'I didn't see her in the carriage just now.'

'She got off at Diss,' said Tim. 'Her shift finished there.' Greg scribbled a note and glanced at Chris.

'I'll have a word,' she said, and went to the back of the carriage, taking out her phone.

Over the muffled sounds of the conversation Greg continued, 'When did you check tickets in First Class?'

'Between Colchester and Manningtree, then again after Diss. Also as normal.'

'Did anyone get on or off at Diss, as well as Janice, I mean?'

'Not from First Class. I think there were a few from Standard.'

'When did you notice a problem with the passenger in Coach C?'

'When Sergeant Mathews called me. I noticed he had his head down, but a lot of people take a nap on the train, so I thought no more about it until the sergeant gave me a shout.'

Chris rejoined them and said briefly as she sat down, 'They're checking.'

Greg nodded. 'What happened then?'

'The sergeant took his pulse in his neck, here,' – he demonstrated on his own neck – 'and said he wasn't breathing. I helped her get him down into the aisle, and she started CPR while I got on the radio. Then I fetched the

defib from the buffet car, we tried that and nothing. It was obvious he'd gone. That was when Sergeant Mathews said to keep the train doors closed until we knew help was ready on the platform. So that's what I told the driver.'

'Where's the driver now?' asked Greg.

'Still in his cab, I should think, waiting for instructions.'

'Okay. We'll have a chat with him later. What else can you tell me about the casualty?'

'Nothing much. He showed me his ticket on his phone, and that was about the extent of my contact with him.'

'How well do you know Janice?'

'Janice? I've worked with her for a couple of years. We're often on the same service. She lives in Diss with her husband and kids. Teenagers now, I should think. That's all I know really, except she likes Robbie Williams. She's often playing music in her headphones when she's setting up or clearing away.'

'Did you see her with the casualty?'

'No. I was just going through to check Standard Class when she started the trolley service.'

'Did you see anything suspicious around the casualty?'

'Such as?' asked the guard.

'Sorry,' said Greg. 'I know it's a very vague question, but I don't want to prompt you. Just give it some thought and answer as best you can.'

'I guess you mean, did I see anyone look like they could have slipped anything into his coffee? No, I didn't. The only people I saw near him were the sergeant here,' – he indicated Chris – 'and I did notice a woman from Coach B go past to the buffet car, because she went while I was checking tickets. Otherwise, you'll have to rely on the CCTV.'

'Of course!' Greg slapped the side of his head and looked up at the ceiling of the carriage. 'I forgot, these modern trains have it all over the place, don't they? Chris, make sure Ned gets everything.' She nodded, and Greg went on. 'I think that's all for now, Mr Nugent. We'll be in touch after the post-mortem. Can you ask the young couple to come through? They can come together.'

'Fancy a coffee?' asked the guard as he left, then paused with a grin. 'Sorry, was that tactless?'

'A bit,' said Greg with an answering grin. 'And you won't be able to get into the buffet car anyway. The scenes of crime team will be busy in there. But thanks for the thought.'

As Tim Nugent left the carriage, Greg looked at Chris.

'Thoughts?' he said.

'Obviously we're looking either at natural causes or poisoning. Personally, I think it may be poisoning, going on the symptoms, and I think the doc thought so too. If so, then theoretically it could be either suicide or murder, but he didn't behave like someone contemplating suicide and mid train journey from London to Norwich seems an odd place to do it. So, my money's on murder.'

'Any idea what? Any smell of bitter almonds, for example?'

'You've been reading too much Agatha Christie,' scoffed Chris. 'Cyanide doesn't always smell of almonds, and not everyone can smell it when it does!'

Greg grinned. 'It's a pity it's not so easy as on the TV, isn't it? One glance from the all-knowing detective, and a precise mystery poison from the Amazon jungle is diagnosed,' he remarked.

'Whereas many poisons have similar effects. But given the speed, and excluding mystery Amazonian plant extracts, I'd guess something like cyanide or botulinum,' replied Chris.

'Any thoughts, then, on how the poison, if any, was administered?'

'If we're setting on one side the possibility he brought it with him, then that leaves the coffee or the biscuit. At least, I didn't see him consume anything else. The obvious source would be the coffee, especially as he complained it was bitter. But not in the pot, because Janice poured me a drink out of the same pot. So that leaves the cup, or the biscuit. It will be interesting to see what Ned finds.'

'What about the milk and sugar?'

'I didn't see him take any sugar. And the milk was in those little sealed pots.'

There was a long pause, as Chris looked through her notes and Greg checked the emails on his phone.

'No one's very pleased about this interruption to our schedule,' he remarked. The Chief Super is particularly narked that we've been deflected from the "mole" investigation. If you wanted to find a distraction,' he added, 'you couldn't have found a better one. The Almighty won't be pleased either!'

'Even the Chief Constable can't expect me to ignore a dead body at my feet,' protested Chris.

'I'm sure he'll find a way to blame you all the same,' said Greg.

They were interrupted by the arrival of the young couple. Greg rose to wave them into the seats opposite, then resumed his seat. He estimated both to be aged around late-twenties to mid-thirties. The young man was wearing a padded jacket over dark jeans, his partner a sheepskin coat over similar. Both were clutching phones, and the young woman had a capacious tote on one arm.

'Sorry to keep you,' said Greg. 'Can you give me your names and addresses, please?'

'Tony and Karen Warboys,' said the man. 'We live in Acle. We're married. So, it's the same address.' And he gave it.

'Why were you on the train?' asked Chris.

'We were coming back from a day out. I had to go to London for work yesterday, so we made an outing of it. Karen came with me, and after my meeting we saw a show, went shopping this morning, and now we're on our way home.'

'Which show?' asked Greg.

'*Les Misérables*,' replied Karen. Her voice was steady, and if she'd been stressed by the events of the afternoon, it seemed it had passed. If anything, she seemed excited.

'Where was your meeting?'

'In the House of Commons. We both work for the RSPCA; it's how we met. There was a meeting yesterday of APGAW. The All-Party Parliamentary Group for Animal Welfare,' he translated. 'About dog welfare and greyhound racing specifically. That's why I was asked to attend. It was an open meeting, so Karen was able to sit in the public seats, then we went to the hotel and out for the evening.'

'Which hotel?'

'The Premier Inn near Liverpool Street.'

'Did you know the man who was taken ill?' asked Greg.

'No. Never seen him,' said Tony.

'Did you notice anything unusual during the journey?'

'Not until the sergeant here and the guard started doing CPR. Everything else seemed normal.'

'Okay.' Greg paused for thought. 'One other thing, do you mind turning out your pockets and letting us see the contents of your bags? You don't have to say yes at this point, but it would be very helpful if we could rule you out. I assume you have another bag beside this. An overnight bag perhaps?'

'Yes. We left that on the luggage rack next door.' He jerked his head over his shoulder.

'I don't mind you looking,' said Karen, 'if it would help.'

'Thank you. Then, if you'd go with Sergeant Mathews, she'll leave you with one of our forensic team, and as soon as they give you the all-clear, you can go home. Please let us know if you're planning on going further afield.'

'No, it's back to work tomorrow,' said Tony, and Karen nodded. Once they'd left the carriage, Greg gave Ned a quick ring and explained what he wanted.

'I assumed we'd need to do something of the kind,' replied Ned. 'Anything in particular we're looking for, other than a pot of cyanide or botulinum toxin?'

'You've got it,' said Greg.

'We'll take samples of the bag linings too,' said Ned, 'just in case we can pick up any traces. Leave it with me.'

At that moment, Chris returned with the bald-headed man. He arrived with a firm tread and an extended hand.

'Gordon Williams,' he said in the slightly overloud voice of the partially deaf. 'How can I help?'

As Mr Williams and Chris took their seats, a loud clamour was audible from the adjacent carriage. Complaints and expostulations were followed by banging on the intervening door, then the sounds of Bill trying to calm things down and the noise retreated into the distance.

'The knight of the realm,' said Chris with an expression of distaste that wasn't lost on their interviewee.

'He's a bully,' said Mr Williams cheerfully. 'Always was and always will be. And like most bullies, he blows himself up like a puffer fish if he thinks he's being ignored. Take no notice – I never did.'

'You know him?' asked Greg.

'A little, for my sins,' replied the man. 'I worked for the NHS for nearly forty years, first as a lab assistant, then a junior manager and finally as a BUM.'

'A what?' asked Greg, bemused.

'A business unit manager,' explained Mr Williams with a grin. 'It was the highlight of my career, the day I went home to announce *"Great news, I've been promoted to be a BUM"*.' Greg laughed, liking the cheerful man in front of him, despite his professional caution about witnesses.

'And Sir Alexander?' he asked.

'I've met him at conferences. He's very into public naming and shaming, even of quite junior staff, which, personally, I think is completely unacceptable. I heard rumours, in fact, of an official complaint, but I retired six months ago, so I don't get the up-to-date gossip any more.'

'Why were you on the train?' asked Chris.

'Just been to an old colleagues' reunion at the Dutch Church near Liverpool Street Station. You know the sort of thing: Waitrose sandwiches, M&S quiches, warm white wine and lots of reminiscence. It was quite fun, actually. So much so, I missed the train I should have got, and caught this one instead.'

'Did you have any contact with Sir Alexander on the train?'

'No, thank God. Anyway, I'd scarcely come to his notice. Much too lowly. I did have a word with Brett though.' Greg's attention sharpened abruptly.

'The dead man?' he said. 'You knew him?'

'A little, yes. Enough to exchange the time of day anyway. He worked in the NHS too.'

'Where?' asked Chris.

'At the Health and Care Hub in Norwich. He worked in communications. You know, writing staff newsletters and the like. I've met him a few times, enough to say hello, as I said, but not well enough that we'd share the journey. Anyway, it was obvious the seat opposite him was taken.' He nodded at Chris. 'So after we said hello and how are you, I went and sat where there was an empty seat further back. The only other time I spoke to him was when I went to the buffet car to fetch a coffee. I paused for a little chat then too, but only for a moment or two, then I saw this lady coming back to her seat and I moved on.'

'What did you chat about?' asked Greg.

'Oh, just the training course he'd been on, only for a moment, as I said, then I went back to my seat.'

'Why didn't you wait for the trolley?' asked Chris.

'I began to wonder if it was going to happen at all,' he replied. 'I waited a while, but I was thirsty after all the white wine, and went to fetch it myself. Of course, shortly after I did the trolley came round, but by then I'd got what I wanted.'

'Do you know anything about Mr Wallace's personal life?' asked Greg. 'You know, like his address, his family and so on?'

'No details,' replied Mr Williams. 'I think he lived in Thorpe St Andrew, or somewhere round there, and I'm fairly sure he was divorced. But that's about all I know.'

***

After leaving Mr Williams with the forensic team for the final check, Chris returned with the final two priority interviewees. 'Mr Wentworth and Ms Hendry,' she said.

Mr Wentworth was a tall, thin man with a goatee beard and ginger hair. His colleague was a chunky woman in middle age with dark bobbed hair, dressed rather elegantly in a tailored navy suit and white jumper. *Country Casuals,* was Chris's silent diagnosis, *or similar.*

'Are we correct in assuming you are colleagues?' asked Greg.

'Correct,' said Ms Hendry, her speech as crisp as her suit.

'Where do you work?'

'French and Sons, Solicitors,' she replied.

'And you were in London because...?'

'To brief counsel on a fraud case. Richard, my assistant, and I have been dealing with a rather complicated case involving embezzlement and probably money laundering as well.'

A few more questions, and it very rapidly became apparent that Richard would be unlikely to speak at all, if his boss was present, and that Ms Hendry had kept both their noses firmly to the grindstone for the entire journey. Neither of them had taken in anything beyond their laptops until the CPR administration had begun, and very little after that until asked to vacate their seats. Once they too were despatched to forensics, Greg leaned back with a sigh.

'This is getting tedious,' he complained. 'And frankly, unless we find the toxic equivalent of a smoking gun, it's unlikely to get us any further forward until we know more about our victim. Come on, let's get the last few out of the way, and then make tracks for Mr Brett Wallace's home.'

'On that,' said Chris, 'I've made a call to his employers. His boss will meet us at Wymondham tomorrow morning, and I have his home address in Gorleston. According to their HR team he lives alone, so I've asked uniform to whip round there and make sure everything is secure.'

'Next of kin?' asked Greg.

'The HR team say he's still got his estranged wife listed as next of kin. She lives in Muswell Hill, London. I haven't done anything about notifying her yet.'

'Okay. That's fine. Let's organise that now, then we can get on with our last few interviews here. So, we have still to go: the knight of the realm, the lady in the red cap, the lad in jeans and beanie I'd put good money on being a dotcom millionaire, and the older couple.'

'Which do you want first?' asked Chris.

'I know who I'd like last, but that would be petty. Take their names, then we'll see them in alphabetical order of surname. That's fair.' Chris grinned and left with her iPad.

3

The remaining passengers

Chris returned from Coach B after only a few minutes. 'We have,' she declaimed, 'Ms Frances Lyell, Frank 'Call-Me-Frankie' Nesbitt, Sir Alexander Smythe, and Mr and Mrs Nigel Craddock. That makes our interview order: Craddock, Lyell, Nesbitt, Smythe; but when I announced that, the entire company rose up as one and pleaded with me to see the great man first, if it was all the same to us. I said I'd check with you.'

'Has he been handing out bribes?' enquired Greg.

'More likely, they can't face sharing space with him any longer. We'll see him next?'

'Okay,' said Greg. 'Let's get it over with.'

Sir Alexander came in with an air of 'And about time too!' He gave his name, with full title and following letters, and his London address in Hampstead, then sighed heavily. Greg surveyed him for a few moments: a florid complexion spoke of too many formal dinners, and a tight waistcoat ditto under a tweed jacket.

Tweed for country, pinstripe for city, thought Greg with an inward smile. The hands currently clasped on the table before him were well manicured, reminding Greg that the rather pompous knight had started out as a well-regarded surgeon.

'I'm sorry to have kept you,' said Greg slightly mendaciously. 'Hopefully we won't be too long now. We have just a few questions, then we'll hand you over to the forensic team for a few simple tests, for exclusionary purposes.'

The knight looked like objecting, then subsided grumpily. 'Let's get it over with then,' he said. 'As I keep telling you, I have a meeting to go to.'

'What did you know of the deceased?' asked Greg, cutting to the chase.

'Nothing at all, except he was apparently a fellow traveller to Norwich.'

'You didn't recognise him?'

'Certainly not. Should I have done?'

'He worked in the NHS,' said Greg.

'And so do almost o=one and a half million others,' replied Sir Alexander. 'You surely don't expect me to know them all!'

'I just asked the question,' pointed out Greg. 'It's a reasonable question. Okay, we've established you didn't know him. What did you see of him during the journey?'

'Again, nothing. We weren't even sitting in the same carriage. Can I go now?'

'In a little,' replied Greg, and exchanged glances with Chris. She took over.

'Where were you today?' she asked.

'At a conference, if that has any relevance to your enquiry. An NHS conference.'

'Where and between what times?'

'I was the keynote speaker. It was at the QEII Centre, and I was there between, oh around ten and two. I had lunch there, then came on to Liverpool St Station to catch this train. I had a meeting at half past six with the local CCG – Clinical Commissioning Group,' he explained. 'But I'll never get to it now. It'll have to be rearranged, and that's a great nuisance. My diary's pretty full.'

'What was the conference? I mean, what was the subject matter?'

'World-class commissioning,' replied Sir Alexander. Feeling none the wiser, Chris made a note. 'Did you go to the buffet car during the journey?'

'No. I always wait for the trolley. It was late, as usual, but it came in the end.'

Chris looked at Greg. 'In that case, I don't think we need keep you any longer,' said Greg. 'Sergeant Mathews will hand you over to our forensic team. I take it you have no objection to cooperating with their tests?'

'What sort of tests?' asked Sir Alexander, looking uneasy for the first time.

'A DNA swab. I'm sure you're familiar with the process. And a check on your luggage and so on. Nothing too intrusive. Everyone else has been happy to assist.'

Sir Alexander blew his cheeks out. 'Well, I suppose so,' he said. 'If I must. But I hope they'll be careful with my papers.'

'They'll be careful,' said Greg, meaning something slightly different, and nodded a farewell.

When Chris got back to Greg she was on fire. 'Something rang a bell, so I checked with Ned. Brett Wallace's wallet had a ticket stub for the cloakroom at the QEII Centre. I think we might find he was at the same conference as our knight of the realm.'

Greg looked up sharply. 'Well, well,' he said. 'I'm looking forward to our chat with Brett Wallace's employers tomorrow morning. Let's have the patient Craddocks in next.'

The Craddocks were retired teachers. Both were, if anything, excited by the unexpected drama added to their trip to Norfolk to visit relatives. Both, equally obviously, were feeling a degree of guilt about enjoying an event which had ended in someone's death. They were keen to help but didn't have much to contribute. Neil Craddock, light brown hair now thinning, and waist thickening, gave his occupation as 'retired deputy head'. His wife, Joy, snazzy in grey trousers and acrylic grey fur jacket, let slip the information that it was of a small primary school, and added that she had been head of maths at a London academy. This minor, and apparently unmalicious, jostling for pre-eminence seemed an endemic trait of their marriage. It came up again when they explained how they planned to spend their time while visiting their son and daughter-in-law in Dereham. Neil was apparently planning to play golf off a more than respectable handicap, while Joy was hoping to meet up with a novelist friend at the Assembly Rooms.

Dragged back to the subject of the fatality, they both had to admit they hadn't seen much of the man on the journey.

'I did go to the buffet car,' said Joy.

'But you got your timing all wrong,' replied Neil. 'The trolley arrived not long after you got back.'

'Well, so you say,' said Joy, 'but I was lucky to get served at all. There was only one attendant, and she closed the counter just after she served me in order to do the trolley service.'

'That's right,' said Neil. 'The trolley didn't come through until we were well on our way, and then it was only hot drinks and biscuits. Sir Whatsit Big-Noise asked her something about proper food and she waved the basket of biscuits at him, but that was all there was. I could have done with a sandwich,' he said with a note of grievance in his voice and his wife chipped in.

'You don't *need* any extra carbs, Neil.' He grimaced at what seemed to be a regular comment.

'Did you notice anything about the casualty?' asked Chris.

'I'm afraid not,' admitted Joy. 'I was too busy balancing two coffees and bottles of water.'

When Chris got back from conveying them to the forensic team, Greg said, 'Hang on a second before we get our next interviewee. Do you remember her walking past you?'

'Not really,' replied Chris. 'I was vaguely aware of people going past but that was all.'

'Looking back at your statement, something else occurs to me,' added Greg. 'You said he "sat down and put his phone in front of him". And Tim Nugent says he checked his ticket on his phone app. But there's no phone now, is there? When did it disappear do you think?'

'Damn! I should have thought of that!' said Chris, chagrined. 'The most obvious opportunity would have been when I went to the loo. But, on the other hand, you'd think he'd have noticed and made a fuss if the phone had disappeared off the table. He was conscious and apparently well for some time after I got back to my seat.'

'Did you notice him using his phone?'

'No, sorry. I was concentrating on my iPad. I can't say, one way or the other.'

'Okay, let's have our next interviewee. It's the lady in the cap, isn't it?'

Frances Lyell was tall and elegant in a tight-fitting, black leather skirt, black jumper and cream puffa jacket. The, somewhat incongruous, red cap was still in evidence on her shiny dark bob. Greg felt that it would have been entirely fitting in the chorus line of *Les Misérables* but looked a little odd in the context of the rest of her outfit. On the other hand, he was used to uncoordinated and vari-coloured outfits on the woman he loved, so he shrugged mentally and waved her to a seat.

She was composed, quiet-voiced and still, except for her hands, which she waved a lot as she talked.

'I just fancied a day out,' she explained. 'It was my treat to myself. I visited the National Portrait Gallery, had a trip on the Thames, then a wander round the Tower of London before getting the train home. All the touristy things you never do when you work in London.'

'Where do you work?' asked Chris.

'At the Defra regional office in Norwich.'

'Were you working for Defra when you worked in London?'

'That's right. I transferred about eighteen months ago.'

'Where do you live?'

'In Reedham.' She gave the address, and Greg noted she was only a few miles from his own home on the river Bure.

'Family?' asked Chris.

'Not here, no. My mother retired to Spain when my father died. I have no brothers or sisters.'

'Husband, or partner?' asked Greg.

'No.'

They went through the now routine questions about any contact with the deceased and got the same negative response as from Sir Alexander. Ms Lyell departed for the forensic checks as Greg and Chris moved on.

***

Frankie Nesbitt, the beanie-clad jeans-wearer was indeed 'in IT' as he put it. Probably no more than thirty, he looked younger – his dyed brown and purple dreadlocks in constant danger of falling over his face. Greg wondered, idly, why he didn't tie them back. He was accompanied by a strong aroma of exotic perfume, which made Chris sneeze. Although eager to help, it seemed that 'Call-Me-Frankie' Nesbitt had little to add to the investigation, until he was about to leave. Then he paused and turned.

'There is one thing,' he said, producing a huge mobile phone from a capacious jacket pocket and waving it. 'I run a subscription service, and one of the things it does, is tell me when a subscriber is in my vicinity. According to this, there were two on the train today. One went off-screen around Diss, so presumably they got off there. The other is still around according to my app. It might be your victim's.'

'That begs a lot of questions,' responded Greg. 'What sort of subscription service? And can you locate the phone?'

'A dating app,' replied Frankie, peering at Greg through the obscuring dreadlocks falling across his face. 'And yes, I can get reasonably close to a location. I'd say it's on the train anyway. That's why I thought it might perhaps be your victim. He seems the right target age and type for the app. The subscriber IDs are encrypted so I can't give you a name, only a code number. But I thought it worth mentioning.'

'Can you take us to where you think the phone is?' asked Greg. 'There wasn't one on the victim. It would be very helpful to find it.'

'Sure thing,' the young man replied and stood to move back down the carriage toward the buffet car. Near the toilets at the end of the carriage, he stopped and looked round, holding his phone in the air. 'Somewhere near here,' he said. 'On the train or nearby on the platform.'

'Tell Ned,' said Greg to Chris, then took Frankie back to the last carriage. 'Now,' he said, 'tell me more about this subscription service of yours.'

'It's a friendship app,' replied Frankie, pushing dreadlocks out of his eyes. 'People sign up with their personal details and preferences, then the underpinning algorithms identify good matches and set them up for a meeting. It even sets up the location for the meeting. All the clients have to do is tap yes, then turn up. Once both parties have tapped yes, the app will show them when the phones are nearby. But only then. I'm the only one who can see all users, because I have the master account and controller rights.'

'And two of your clients were showing up on your screen earlier in the journey, but one got off at Diss.'

'That's right.'

'Do you have the IDs for the clients who show up on your app?' asked Chris.

'I have the IDs for all clients on the database,' replied Frankie, pushing his hair back again. 'But not on the app map. That's to preserve client confidentiality.'

'When do clients find out the ID of their matches?' enquired Greg.

'They get first names and a few details, like age, occupation and so on, when the algorithm matches them up. Then when they've both tapped yes, they get a few more, like home location – in general terms, say county or city – and hobbies. And the phone of their matchee will show up on their app map when they're close enough – say, on the same mast signal. That way, they can check their date is actually in the vicinity for the first meeting, but they can't spy on their movements from a distance. It's very safe,' he assured them. Reserving his private thoughts, Greg thanked him and passed him on for the forensic tests.

Chris got to her feet. 'I'll see how Ned's getting on with finding that phone,' she said, but was interrupted by Bill waving in the doorway.

'We've got it,' he said.

4

Next steps

The following morning saw both Greg and Chris in the police HQ in Wymondham bright and early. Even so, the post-mortem report was already in Greg's emails.

'Dr Paisley must have started early,' remarked Chris.

'Yes, she said she was aiming for a 7 am start,' replied Greg, still reading the report. 'I asked if I should be there, but she said she didn't think she'd have much to show me: that the verdict would probably depend on analytical chemistry. This...' – he tapped the screen – 'says her preliminary conclusion is cause of death was cyanide poisoning. She'll confirm later when she gets more test results back, but she doesn't expect that to be overturned.'

'So it must have been the coffee,' said Chris. 'Cyanide is quick. It was probably either the coffee or something he took with the coffee. Any signs he may have had it with him?'

'Nothing. Nothing either the doc or Ned can find, anyway. So, let's assume it was administered by someone in or with the coffee. How could they have done it?'

Chris started to make a list on her notepad. 'In the coffee itself? No, because, as I already said, I had coffee from the same pot. That leaves the cyanide:

- *already in the cup when the coffee was poured,*
- *in one of the bags of sugar,*
- *in one of the pots of milk,*
- *in a biscuit,*
- *slipped into his coffee after it was poured.*

Of those, we can rule out the last.' She drew a decisive line through the phrase on her page. 'I would have seen that, but we can check the CCTV to make sure.'

'Rule out the biscuit too,' said Greg. 'Dr Paisley says there's no sign he ate anything immediately prior to his death.'

Chris deleted another line. 'That leaves the cup, the sugar and the milk, which all point towards—'

'The buffet-car attendant who got off at Diss. I've got uniform bringing her in for questioning this morning. We've got even more questions to ask now. But first, let's see Brett Wallace's boss and see what we can learn about our victim.'

'Of course,' said Chris, 'the other possibility we shouldn't rule out is me. Arguably I could have slipped something into his coffee.'

'True, if you've taken up murdering random strangers as a hobby. Have you, as a matter of interest?'

'No. But we should follow the rules. You can't just assume it wasn't me.'

'True,' said Greg again. 'But I'm ahead of you. I've already asked Ned to check the CCTV footage. He says one of the cameras has your seat clearly in shot. He's been through the footage up to and immediately after the coffee was served. He can see Wallace taking a drink from his coffee. And he says you're in the clear. According to him you didn't even drag your attention from your iPad to look at your own drink, let alone put anything in his.'

'Thank goodness for that,' said Chris.

***

Michael Wilson, CEO of Norfolk Health and Care, was smart of both dress and intelligence. Tall, slim and dark-haired, he was a good advert for healthy living. He was already sitting in the interview suite when joined by Greg and Chris and got to his feet as they entered the room. He towered over them both – an unusual experience for Greg – and shook hands with a slight stoop, as though trying to diminish his height.

'This is terrible,' he said. 'I'm so shocked. I would have said Brett was a man without enemies. Do you think it was some dreadful mistake?'

'We're keeping an open mind at present,' said Greg. 'Do take a seat, and thank you for coming in. I must admit, when we asked to see Mr Wallace's immediate superior, I didn't expect it to be the CEO.'

'It's the way we're organised,' explained Michael Wilson. 'By the way, do please call me Michael. The communications team report directly to me, and Brett was the head of it. Very good he was too. We'll find him difficult to replace. He wrote well, he was proactive, and he wasn't afraid to stand up and say the unpopular when necessary. I still can't quite take it in. His death, I mean!'

'Did saying the unpopular make *him* unpopular?' asked Greg. 'Did he have any enemies you're aware of?'

'No, and no,' replied Michael. 'By that comment, I meant he would say if he disagreed with a policy, or, more likely, how a policy was being expressed to staff. I found that very helpful. The last thing a CEO needs in that role is a yes-man. He was also willing to stand up for more junior staff; as when he made a formal complaint about a bigwig. I respected that and I know the juniors did.'

'Which bigwig?' asked Greg with a premonition that he already knew the answer.

'Alexander Smythe. Brett lodged a complaint that he had bullied junior staff.'

'Was it upheld?' asked Chris.

'It's still going through the system. I think it probably will be, or would have been, if Brett were around to see the process through. Hang on,' he added suddenly. 'You don't suspect Sir Alexander do you? He didn't turn up to a CCG meeting last night. And he could have been on that train. No, I don't think he'd do anything like that. He's not a nice man, but I don't think he's homicidal. It would be beneath him.'

'As I said, we're keeping our minds open,' said Greg. 'But what can you tell me about Brett Wallace as a man? What do you know about his personal life?'

'Only a little,' replied Michael. 'He lived in Thorpe St Andrew. I know we've already given you his address. He was separated from his wife. She moved back to London, I think. But, as far as I know, they haven't divorced yet. The last time we had a conversation about her, he said she'd put him off marriage for life, so there was no reason for him to fork out for a divorce. If she wanted one, that was up to her. He hadn't gone off women altogether though. He told me he'd tried a dating app. But that's all I know.'

Once Michael Wilson had been shown out by a civilian assistant, Chris and Greg looked at each other.

'Our knight was being a bit disingenuous,' remarked Chris. 'Not only were they both at the same conference that day, but Wallace had lodged a formal complaint against him. It beggars belief that he wouldn't have known who Wallace was.'

'Hard to see how he would have administered the cyanide though,' said Greg. 'But we certainly need another word with the knight. Where was he staying in Norwich?'

'The Maids Head, of course,' replied Chris.

'Okay, let's see if we can pick him up from there before he disappears for his day's meetings or back to London. Can you get someone there asap?'

'On it,' said Chris, and hurried out of the room. Greg had barely sat down at his desk again when Bill stuck his head round the door.

'Janice Jones is here,' he said. 'The buffet-car attendant. And in a bit of a flap.'

'Okay. I'll see her as soon as Chris gets back.'

'Oh, and she's asked for a solicitor,' added Bill.

'Her own or the duty one?'

'Duty,' said Bill. 'Shall I set it up?'

'Yes, please. In that case, there's no immediate hurry. Tell them we'll be down in an hour.'

***

It was apparent, when Greg and Chris entered the interview room, that young Mr Carlow had succeeded in calming his agitated client. Although still twisting a damp hanky in her hands, the middle-aged blonde sitting next to the youthful solicitor was, at least, no longer in floods of tears.

'I've told my client,' said Mr Carlow, slightly self-importantly, 'that she should cooperate with your questioning, as she has nothing to hide.'

Privately Greg wondered if a more experienced solicitor would have adopted the same strategy but chose not to look a gift horse in the mouth. 'I'm grateful for your assistance,' he said. 'Just to explain the process, Mrs Jones, I will shortly begin the tape recording and will ask you and your solicitor to identify yourselves. Then I'll administer the caution – you'll have heard it on TV, I'm sure – and then we'll get down to the questions about the journey yesterday. Is that clear?'

Janice Jones nodded nervously, then said, 'Yes.'

The formalities out of the way, the witness looked, if anything, even more petrified than before. Greg nodded to Chris to start with the easy questions.

'We spoke to your colleague Tim Nugent yesterday,' she began. 'Have you worked with him before? Sorry, I should have asked, is it okay if I call you Janice?'

'Yes,' said Janice. 'And yes, I work with Tim regularly. Have done for at least a couple of years.'

'Talk me through what happened on your shift yesterday,' said Chris.

'What, all of it?' asked Janice. 'From when I first started in the morning?'

'No. Just your time on the 4 pm from Liverpool Street,' replied Chris.

'Okay. Well, I joined the train as normal about fifteen minutes before it was due to leave. I spent the time sorting out the buffet car, and found out I was, as so often these days, working the journey on my own. There should be two of us,' she added, 'but often there isn't. If there's two, then one does the counter work and the other does the trolley, but with only one...' She shrugged.

'What did you do?'

'I opened the counter shortly after we left. The Tim made an announcement that because of a shortage of staff there would be a limited counter and trolley service, so there was a bit of a rush of Standard Class passengers collecting coffees and so on. I did that until the Ipswich stop, then I closed the counter and rushed through the trolley service for First Class. Just hot drinks, biscuits and crisps. I didn't have time for anything else. There was one complaint about no proper food service, but most people on that train aren't expecting a meal service anyway.'

'Who complained?' asked Greg.

'A big chap in tweeds. Red in the face and a loud voice.' Greg and Chris had no difficulty identifying Sir Alexander Smythe from that description.

'So, you went round with coffee and tea. What do you remember about serving the man who was taken ill?'

'Not much to be honest. I'm told it was a man in Coach C, but I was in a bit of a rush, and I just poured out teas and coffees as asked. Milk and sugar were already on the tables.'

'Hold on,' said Chris. 'Go back a bit. When did you put the milk and sugar out?'

'I didn't,' replied Janice. 'I had a basket of each on my trolley, but they were already out on the tables. I assumed the last crew must have left them there. I didn't stop to think about it. As I said, I was in a rush, so I just poured the drinks, went back to the buffet car, tidied up and got off at Diss.'

Greg passed Chris a note.

Check the CCTV.

She nodded and left the room.

'Sergeant Mathews has left the room,' said Greg for the tape. 'Janice, did you recognise anyone on the train that day? Passengers, I mean.'

'There were some regulars in Standard,' she replied. 'One or two said hello when they came to the buffet car. That was all. No one in First.'

'Did you notice anything about the passengers in Coach C?'

'No, as I said, I was too busy rushing about.'

'And you definitely didn't put the milks and sugars out on the tables?'

'No. I already said: they were already there.'

Chris came back in and slid a note in front of Greg.

Sugars and milks clearly visible on the table before the trolley arrived.

Greg nodded.

'Okay. Then I think that's it for now, Mrs Jones. We'll be in touch if we need to ask you anything else.'

***

Back in his office, Greg reached for the phone. 'We need Jill's expertise on CCTV,' he said, then added into the phone, 'Jill, can you pop along to my office please, I need your help.' Constable Jill Hayes came in within a few minutes, already aware of the likely reason for the request.

'The CCTV,' she said. 'I've already been taking a preliminary look.'

'Yes. I'm sorry, Jill, but it needs a close scrutiny for the whole of the journey from London to Norwich. In particular, we need to know how and when the sugar and milk portions arrived on the tables in First Class, what happened to the victim's phone, and anything else you can turn up about contacts with the victim during the journey.

'No problem,' said Jill. 'Leave it with me.' And she hurried away.

'Okay. Now that's underway, let's get ourselves over to Thorpe St Andrew and see what we can learn about our victim.'

Twenty minutes later, they drew up before the impressive frontage of a Grade II listed building. 'What was this?' asked Greg. 'If it was a house, it was enormous!'

'It was a hospital, I think,' said Chris, grovelling in the bottom of her puce tote for her notebook. 'Yes, St Andrew's Hospital. These buildings date from the 1800s and apparently "have been tastefully converted into townhouses".' She dropped the estate agent's style and added, 'Brett Wallace had an apartment on the top floor. We've got a man on the door upstairs.'

Leaving his car next to the liveried police car at the front door, earning a glare from another resident in the process, Greg followed Chris into the lobby and up the grand staircase to the upper floor. Brett Wallace's apartment turned out to have an elegant kitchen-diner, a living room, two bedrooms and a bathroom, all with solid wood floors, pale walls and views over the park. Everywhere was tidy, except for the film of fingerprint powder and the signs of a thorough search.

'Ned gone?' Greg asked Steve on the door.

'Just now. He's taken a couple of things with him, in particular a laptop. He said to tell you that he'd let you have an analysis of its contents asap, but, as far as he could see, the main area of interest was his membership of a dating site.'

'Ah,' said Greg, and Chris flipped through her notebook again.

'Our internet whizzkid from yesterday said he thought Wallace might be one of his customers. We need to follow that up.'

'We do,' said Greg. 'Where's he based?'

'Not far away. Just round the corner from Norwich City football ground.'

'Okay. Let's go there next. Anything else of interest here, Steve?'

'Nothing out of the ordinary, except he seems to have been a lot tidier than most. The place was immaculate when we arrived: dishwasher contents clean, pretty much everything else put away or, in the case of clothes, in a laundry basket. He wasn't one to leave stuff on the floor.'

'Any signs anyone else lived here?'

'None. Only one set of stuff in the bathroom, the spare bedroom seems to have been used as a study, and all the clothes in the cupboards seem to have been his.'

Chris had been looking round the walls and turned to say, 'Nothing much in the way of personal photos either. The big photos in here are all of the Broads. There are a couple of old theatre posters, reproductions I think, in the kitchen, and the only personal photo looks like one of his parents in the bedroom.' She looked closer at one of the big photos and added, 'He may have taken this himself. He's signed the mount. Did you find any cameras?'

'Yes, we did,' said Steve. 'In the spare bedroom-cum-study. We found a will too.'

'Who benefits?' asked Greg.

'Two nieces and a couple of cousins. The solicitor who drew it up is a local too.'

'In that case, let's ask him for any background on the will. He'll need to be informed anyway.'

'She,' said Steve. 'The solicitor is a she. A Fiona Harrison of French and Sons.'

'That rings a bell—' started Chris.

'Same firm as our two on the train: Ms Hendry. More coincidence!' said Greg

They ran Frankie Nesbitt to earth in his first-floor offices above a bicycle shop. As far as they could see, there were three rooms and two employees plus Frankie, but that was a misapprehension, as he swiftly explained.

'Kate here looks after reception and, since very few of our customers come to the office, she also does the accounts. Jamie, the occupant of the second room, is the expert who keeps us up and running, and he set up all our security – fire walls and so on. I do the development, and a team of home workers operate remotely to process applications, review matches, update online entries, chase up reviews and so on.

'But you didn't come here to learn how a dating business works. You wanted to know whether any of my customers were on that train. Come through, and I'll tell you what I've been able to find out.' He sat them down in his office, offered coffee, then reached for a keyboard. 'This is what I found out for you earlier,' he said, tapping in a password, then staring fixedly at a camera. Chris started to say something, but he waved for silence, held an unsmiling pose for a second then turned to them.

'Sorry,' he said. 'Because of the need for data protection, I use two-factor security. Both a password and facial recognition. The latter is a bit temperamental. I need to sit very still for the camera. Anyway, this is what I can tell you.

'First, Brett Wallace *was* a customer. He had been on three dates set up by our app, but if he met any of the women again, he didn't tell us. I assume you'll want the names and addresses.'

'Yes, please,' said Greg.

'I'll print them off. One is a Londoner, the other two live in Norfolk. Before I do, though, can you assure me that you won't misuse the information or leak it to the press. That would play merry hell with my business.'

'It will be used only for the purposes of our investigation,' Greg assured him. 'And why on earth should you think we'd leak anything to the press?'

'If you're asking me that, I take it you haven't seen the Eastern Daily Press today?'

'No,' said Greg.

Frankie tapped a few keys on a different keyboard, then waved Greg to a second screen. The image was of an obviously irate Sir Alexander being pushed into a police car outside the Maids Head Hotel, and the caption suggested that he was 'helping police with their enquiries' into a murder on the Norwich Express. The implication was that this revelation was an 'exclusive', courtesy of an informant.

'Whoops,' said Chris tactlessly.

Greg glared at her and said, 'I think that's a classic case of the press adding two and two and making five. You can be sure they won't hear about your customers from us, unless of course we charge any of them with an offence.'

Frankie shrugged. 'Well, they say all publicity is good publicity, don't they? Here you are.' He reached round and took a sheet of paper from the printer behind him. 'These are the three contacts he made through us.'

Lindsay Jenkin. 26, Pages Lane, Muswell Hill
Sophie Gough. 21, The Street, Aylsham
Frances Lyell. The Oaks, Reed Street, Reedham.

'Well, bless me,' said Greg slowly. 'Our lady in the Les Mis cap.'

5

Enlisting help

After due consultation with the boss, it was decided to enlist some help from colleagues in London. A detective inspector and detective constable duly made their way to Pages Lane, Muswell Hill. Turning in past the Methodist Hostel, they were surprised to note that the two addresses they were to visit were exactly opposite each other.

'What's the odds on that?' asked DI Martin Crews of his assistant, DC Sally DeMenez.

'Very handy. His ex-wife just across the road from a new squeeze.' DeMenez shook glossy black hair from her face, where the rain had stuck it to her glasses, and strode up to the front door of 26, Pages Lane. An overweight, middle-aged gentleman age answered the door, hoisting his trousers up over a well-developed paunch to reveal bare ankles above suede lace ups.

'Yes,' he said. 'What can I do for you?' Both officers held out their warrant cards.

'May we speak to Lindsay Jenkin, sir,' said Martin Crews.

'You may, always supposing you can find her and she's not a figment of someone's imagination,' replied the gent. 'I've never met her, and if you can stop dating agencies sending their material here, I'd be very grateful.' And with that, he closed the door. Martin banged on it again, and after a considerable delay it reopened.

'I've told you—' began the man.

'I don't think you understand, sir,' said Martin. 'I am Detective Inspector Crews, and we are investigating a murder. This address has been connected with the investigation, and I'm sure you'd rather answer a few friendly questions here than come down to the station and answer them under caution.'

'Oh for goodness' sake, come in then, and let's have an end to it,' snapped the man.

He led them into an overfurnished front room and threw himself into an armchair by the unlit fire. 'What do you want to know?'

'Your name would be a good place to start,' said Constable DeMenez.

'Frederick Neame,' he replied.

'Occupation?'

'Headteacher at the school just down the road.'

'Are you married, Mr Neame?'

'Yes. But I won't be much longer if my wife is given any more reason to think I'm going on dating sites.'

'You say you don't know a Lindsay Jenkin?' DI Crews picked up the questioning.

'Never heard of her, until a few months ago, when correspondence started arriving here addressed to her.'

'And what about Friends Inc?'

'Again, never heard of them until I got their adverts coming through the door addressed to this Jenkin person. We laughed it off to start with, but as they kept coming my wife started to make comments about avatars and people masquerading as members of the opposite sex. Then the comments became barbed jokes in company, so now, if anything arrives for LJ, I bin it straight away and hope she won't see it.'

Crews and DeMenez exchanged glances. Then DeMenez asked, 'Do you know your neighbour across the road, Mr Neame?'

'Susie? Just to say hello to, no more than that. Susie Wallace I think her name is, but you know how it is. When it comes to taking in parcels for neighbours and so on, it tends to be for the ones next door rather than the ones over the road.'

'I see.' Crews came to a swift decision. 'Thank you, Mr Neame. It seems there may have been some misunderstanding. If we have any more questions, we'll be in touch.'

Neame showed them to the door, then watched, puzzled, as they walked past their car and to the door of No 15 opposite. Another ring at another doorbell. Another delay, and then the door opened slowly on a woman with red eyes clutching a box of tissues.

'Come in,' she said. 'Is this about Brett again?'

This sitting room, in structure a mirror image of the one over the road, was minimalist to the point of being bare. The floorboards were exposed and clearly showed where there had previously been a carpet. Two armchairs were supplemented by a sofa that probably belonged in a conservatory, and a matching bamboo table with a worn rattan top.

'Would you like tea or coffee?' she asked. 'I'm afraid I don't have any milk but you're welcome, if you can drink it black.' Both declined the offer, and again showed their warrant cards as they introduced themselves. 'I've already had the news you know,' she said. 'A young constable came to see me yesterday to tell me my husband was dead. And the solicitors rang this morning to say he'd cut me out of his will, so I can't imagine there's much more bad news to come.'

'It wasn't about that,' said DI Crews. 'I wanted to ask you about another matter. What do you know about Lindsay Jenkin?'

There was a petrified silence lasting several minutes, then Mrs Wallace leaned back in her chair. She put a hand wearily to her brow and replied, 'I suppose it doesn't matter now. Lindsay Jenkin was me.'

On the phone to Greg, Martin Crews explained, 'She says it was an attempt to get them back together. She says she never wanted them to split up, but Brett couldn't forgive what she called "her little mistakes" and moved out to take a new job in Norfolk. I asked what the little mistakes were. Had she been unfaithful, for example? She said no, nothing like that, just lost her temper a few times when she'd been under stress. I couldn't get any more out of her than that, but I'm guessing, for him to react like that, that he might have been subjected to domestic abuse. It wouldn't be too difficult to check.'

'What about her whereabouts during that afternoon, when Brett Wallace died on the train to Norwich?'

'At work in the estate agents in Muswell Hill. That checks out. We called in, and both the manager and a fellow worker say she was working that afternoon. No way she could have been on that train. There's supporting paperwork on their system too.'

'Did you find out if he met with "Lindsay Jenkin"?' asked Greg.

'Not according to Mrs Wallace. She says they arranged to meet for drinks in the bar at the Strand Palace and that the app showed he was in the vicinity. But he never showed up.'

'Probably saw her and realised he'd been conned,' remarked Greg.

'That was my assumption too. I have to say, I felt a bit sorry for her,' added Martin. 'Whatever the rights and wrongs of their relationship, she's clearly struggling financially, and being excluded from his will has been a big blow.'

***

Hardly had Greg put the phone down, than it rang again. His latest interviewee had arrived, and temperatures were rising fast. Greg correctly interpreted that to mean that Sir Alexander Smythe was in the building, and hurried down to see him, scooping up DI Jim Henning on the way.

'You've read the file, Jim?' he asked as they walked briskly down the long corridor to the interview suite. Jim flourished the file under one arm as he pushed the last mouthful of a bacon butty into his mouth with the other hand.

'Yup,' he said somewhat indistinctly.

'Isn't it a bit late for breakfast?' enquired Greg enviously.

'Yup,' said Jim again, swallowing hard. 'But better late than never. There. Ready now. Why did you want me in particular?'

Reflecting ruefully that his breakfast had been 'never', Greg replied, 'I wanted a fresh pair of eyes on this chap. He was so obnoxious on the train I'm not sure Chris can be objective. I'm not sure I can, to be honest. If he'd gone out of his way to be the archetypal self-important, pompous prat he couldn't have done it better. But there must be more. For all its occasional faults, the NHS doesn't generally appoint complete pillocks to that sort of position of responsibility, and his reputation as a surgeon was outstanding. So, I need you to help me get below the outer skin.'

'And he's of interest because of the bullying complaint from the deceased? Anything else?' asked Jim.

'Nothing yet from Ned or the CCTV, but that's because I haven't had *anything* from Ned yet; so it's an absence of evidence, not evidence of innocence. I was just about to chase Ned when this chap arrived.'

Entering the interview room, Greg noted that a senior-looking solicitor had arrived to support Sir Alexander. Introductions and formalities over, the caution administered and the tape running, Greg paused and looked at Sir Alexander for a long moment. The pause was interrupted by the solicitor, one Jacob Isaacs, from the Norwich branch of a London firm. Obviously procured in a hurry.

'Sir Alexander is a busy man with a lot of demands on his time,' he said. 'So I want you to know that, to expedite this process and to waste as little time as possible, I have advised him to cooperate with your questioning.'

Sir Alexander leaned back in his chair and waited. To Greg, his perceptions coloured by experience, he looked as grumpy as ever. To Jim, coming to the man without expectations, he looked ill.

'Thank you,' said Greg. 'I'm sure that will help. And I would like to apologise for the press attention at the Maids Head. I have been told it was the result of an unguarded comment on a police radio that was picked up by the press. It was not our intention to be indiscreet.' Sir Alexander nodded, but said nothing. 'The reason we wish to talk to you,' went on Greg, 'is to explore what you knew about Brett Wallace, and, particularly, why you didn't tell me yesterday that you knew him as the man who had made a formal complaint about you.'

'Because I didn't know,' said Sir Alexander. 'I told you I didn't know him, and that was the truth. As far as I know I've never met him, other than by sitting in the same conference theatre.'

'What was the complaint?' asked Jim.

'That I bullied some junior members of staff during a discussion in a conference. A chap from a community NHS trust gave a damn fool answer to a question I'd asked and I told him as much. Apparently, that was bullying, at least in this man's eyes.'

'I take it the complaint had a name attached. Even if you didn't recognise the man on the train, didn't you recognise the name?' asked Greg.

'Was the name mentioned on the train? I don't recall. And I'm terrible with names. Just ask any of my staff. When I was operating, I always remembered the condition but rarely the name of the person who had it. *That* upset people sometimes too,' he said.

'Had you taken any action against Brett Wallace? In defending yourself against the complaint?'

'Of course not. I left it to others to deal with. Look,' he said, 'when you're in my sort of position, you get complaints. It's routine. You let the system deal with it. Mostly they go away.'

'But this one hadn't gone away, had it? Although it probably will, now the complainant is dead.' The colour rose in Sir Alexander's face and his voice along with it.

'So I'm supposed to have murdered someone to get out of a footling complaint. Don't be ridiculous. Anyway, I had more—' He paused as he intercepted a warning glance from his solicitor.

Jim intervened. 'What were you going to say, Sir Alexander?' he asked. 'That you had more important things on your mind? What were they?'

Another pause as the solicitor nodded, then Sir Alexander said heavily, 'I don't want this going outside this room. I haven't even told my wife yet. I've been diagnosed with cancer of the pancreas. It's probably been making me a bit short-tempered. Or,' he amended with the first flash of humour Greg had seen, 'even shorter-tempered than usual.'

Into the silence the solicitor said, 'I imagine you might want to check with Sir Alexander's specialist. If so, we can supply the name.' Sir Alexander scowled, but nodded.

***

Back in his office, Greg drew a line through Sir Alexander's name on the whiteboard and rang Ned. 'Still no results?' he asked. 'Ned, this is getting a bit pressing.'

'I know,' said the harassed crime scene manager. 'I've been chasing, believe me, but it's taken me until a few moments ago to get any answer at all, let alone any sense. All they can tell me is that they're backed up with priority work and they'll get round to our samples as soon as they can.'

‘And Brett Wallace’s phone? Anything there?’

‘Nothing of interest. Yes, he was on the Friends Inc app, and yes, there was a ping from another member, but we knew that already from the Nesbitt chap.’

‘The CCTV?’ said Greg, hope fading.

‘Still being reviewed. You do realise there are three hours of footage on each of multiple cameras?’

‘Yes, I know. Thanks, Ned. Let me know if I can help at all as regards the laboratory. Chris!’ he bellowed down the corridor. ‘Let’s get over to Aylsham and see this Sophie Gough.’

Sophie turned out to be a buxom early-forties with a warm smile and sharp intelligence. ‘Yes, I did invite a connection from Brett Wallace, and, yes, we did meet up. Twice actually. The first time we had coffee at the Assembly House – my suggestion. I’ve learned from bitter experience to set up the first meeting to be short, and somewhere I like, so if all else fails I can at least enjoy the surroundings.’

‘How did you get on?’ asked Chris. They were interviewing Sophie in her insurance broker office. If she wasn’t the boss, she was clearly senior, judging by the functionally plush surroundings and the pleasant watercolours of the Broads on the wall.

‘Well, I thought. He was interesting to talk to. He listened as well as talked. In fact, unlike a lot of men, he didn’t say all that much about himself. Just that he was divorced, worked in the NHS and lived in Thorpe St Andrew.’

Greg sipped his excellent black coffee. ‘You got on well enough to meet again?’

'That's right. Second time, we agreed we'd have dinner at the Last Wine Bar.' Greg grinned involuntarily at this mention of one of his own favoured eateries.

'What happened after that?' he asked.

'Dinner went well enough. Again, we had lots to chat about and we seemed to have quite a lot in common. We'd just discussed going for a day out in a hire boat from Wroxham when the mad ex showed up.'

'The mad ex?' asked Chris, some fellow-feeling hovering at the back of her mind.

'Yes. The ex, or to be accurate, not-quite-ex wife. We were just on to coffee, when this woman appeared at our table and smacked a pile of envelopes down in front of Brett. She stood there with her back to me, not quite shouting at Brett. I can't remember the precise words, but the gist was: *what was he doing taking fancy women out for dinner when all these bills need to be paid?* I was torn between embarrassment, feeling sorry for him and getting the giggles. It was so like a sitcom it was unreal.'

'What happened next?' asked Chris.

'Brett got up and tried to quieten her down, but that just made her louder. The manager came up and asked her to leave the restaurant as she was disturbing his customers, and Brett went outside with her, very red-faced. I settled the bill and followed them. I was interested to see the next episode,' she added frankly. 'Just plain nosy, really. By the time I got out there, she was marching off down the street. There were bits of paper everywhere, which I deduced to mean she'd torn the bills up and thrown them in his face. He was still red-faced, and one side was redder than the other, so I think she'd clouted him as well. If it was a sitcom,' she added, 'it needed a more original scriptwriter. We said our goodbyes and went our separate ways, me back to the car park in Golden Dog Lane, Brett walking toward the river. I was still laughing when I got in the car, but by the time I got home, I was having second thoughts. I decided that, nice as Brett was, I didn't want to get involved with that sort of baggage. So I rang him the following day and told him I wouldn't be meeting him again.'

'How did he take it?' asked Greg.

'Didn't sound surprised. If anything, I think the only thing that surprised him was me ringing, rather than dumping him by text.'

Back in the car, Greg looked at his watch. 'Okay, back to Norwich and a chat with our rebel from Les Mis. I think we're going to miss lunch, Chris.'

'Probably all to the good,' said Chris with a prod at Greg's slightly rounded tummy. 'I swear this is growing!'

'What, my six-pack?' asked Greg in mock outrage as he started the car. Chris was looking at her phone. 'I've got a message from the office,' she said. 'Ms Lyell has asked if we could see her at or near her office. Says she's busy.'

'Where's the office?' asked Greg.

'Thorpe Rd.'

'Hmm.' He thought, while navigating traffic. 'We've already postponed this conversation to suit her convenience. I wanted the option of interviewing her under caution. After all, she's not only one of Wallace's internet contacts, but she was also on the train.'

'And she didn't say anything about that,' added Chris.

'Okay, tell her we'll interview her at her place of work, provided she can guarantee a private space to do it in. A conference room, say. If it's a shared space, it's not on.'

Frances Lyell was in monochrome again: black fitted dress and a cream scarf with some sort of black print on it. Greg could feel Chris's disapproval from where he was sitting at the far end of the conference table. Chris had her notebook very much in evidence at the head of the table, by the door, and was sorting out her recorder while Frances took her elegant seat opposite Greg.

'Thank you for seeing me here,' she said. 'A trek to Wymondham would have been most inconvenient.'

'No problem,' said Greg. 'As it happens, we were in Norwich already. However, notwithstanding the location, I must make it clear that this is a formal interview under caution. We will be recording it and taking notes.'

'If this is under caution, do I need a solicitor?' enquired Frances.

'That is your right. But, in that case, we will definitely need to adjourn to Wymondham. Your choice.'

'Can I change my mind during the inquisition?' she asked.

'Of course.'

There was a pause while she looked out of the window. 'Okay,' she said finally. 'I may live to regret this, but I'll go along with it for the moment. I don't want to impede your investigation.'

'Thank you.' Greg took a moment to clear his thoughts, then asked, 'Why didn't you tell us, when we interviewed you, that you knew the victim?'

Frances Lyell blinked, then replied, 'Because I didn't want to get involved in anything to do with Brett Wallace.'

'When did you last meet Brett Wallace? I mean, before the train journey?'

'At the Kings Arms in Fleggburgh, a month ago. I can give you the precise date if I check my diary.' At a nod from Greg, she flicked through screens on her phone, then said, 'It was the last Saturday in the month. We met for lunch. I'm sure the King's Arms will confirm.'

'Did you speak to him on the train?'

'No. We were not on speaking terms.'

'Why not? What happened?'

'I told him I didn't want to see him anymore. He didn't take it well.'

'Why did you make that decision? asked Chris, guessing that she knew what was coming next.

'On our previous date, in Norwich at the Theatre Royal, his supposedly ex-wife turned up and made a fuss. We were in the Prelude restaurant, and it was very embarrassing. I also wasn't amused to find out he wasn't divorced after all.'

'How many times had you met before that?' asked Greg.

'Oh, a few times. We had coffee at first in Jarrolds. Then drinks one evening in a pub in Acle. Then the theatre, no, before that we had drinks and supper in a pub in Norwich.

Then the theatre, complete with mad wife, then the Kings Arms.'

'What did you think of him, as a man?' asked Chris.

'I liked him to start with. He was a good listener. He was interested in things I was interested in, like the theatre and books. But he was a bit weak and wet. I really saw that when his wife showed up. And as I said, I thought he was divorced, so it was a bit of a shock to find he wasn't.'

'Did your relationship move on to a more intimate footing?' asked Greg.

'Did I sleep with him, you mean? No, I did not. I'm not that fast a mover!'

'Let's go to the train trip,' said Greg. 'Did you go to the buffet car?'

'No.'

'So, you didn't pass his seat on the train?'

'No.'

'Did you know he was on the train?'

'No. Not until she' – Frances pointed at Chris – 'started bossing everyone around.' Greg suppressed a grin, well aware that Chris regarded bossy as a compliment, not an insult.

'But the app told you he was on the train, didn't it?' he asked.

Frances opened her mouth, closed it again, then said, 'I thought you meant had I seen him in person, rather than just in an app.'

'So you did know he was on the train?'

'Well, the app said he was near, yes.'

‘If you dumped him, why didn’t you block him from your app feed?’ asked Chris.

‘I hadn’t got round to it.’

‘To sum up,’ said Greg after a pause, ‘you did know Brett Wallace was on the train but, because you had parted on poor terms, you didn’t look for him to speak to him, and you didn’t pass his seat during the journey. Did you see him while you were in London that day?’

‘Of course not,’ said Frances with a note of scorn in her voice. ‘Aren’t you listening? We weren’t on speaking terms. Why would I go looking for him?’

Back in the car, Chris and Greg looked at each other. ‘Okay, what have we learned,’ asked Greg. ‘First, the not-quite-ex Mrs Wallace seems to have made a habit of turning up on Brett’s dates. Second, the result in at least two cases seems to have been that his dates dumped him. Questions?’

Chris flicked the pages of her notebook. ‘I’ve a few,’ she said. ‘First, what evidence do we have that either Sophie or Frances did dump him? We’ve only their say-so. Second, how did Mrs Wallace find out about the dates? Third, I think we need to check Mrs Wallace’s alibi.’

6

A new day

A new morning, a new day, and Greg was in a bit of a temper. Chris could see the signs, as could the rest of the office. Most of them were treading warily. Chris opted to stride in where angels would have been a bit cautious.

'What the devil's the matter with you?' she asked. 'You've been in a right old strop all morning.'

'This case,' he said. 'It looked straightforward. It should be straightforward, but I feel I'm walking in the dark. We have a few suspects, but as fast as we check them out, they acquire alibis. The forensic lab seems to have gone on strike as far as our samples are concerned, and there are so many miles of video, even Jill's got bogged down.

'Look.' He went over to the whiteboard. 'This is where I think we've got to. Correct me if I'm wrong or if anything new has come up. In no particular order:

'Sir Alexander Smythe – we've already deleted him. Wallace had made a formal complaint against him re bullying, but there's no reason Sir A should have recognised him in person and the complaint wasn't a big deal when set against his diagnosis of cancer. There's no evidence he went near Wallace on the train, and he didn't go to the buffet car. So, no motive and no means.' He tapped the line already drawn through the knight's name on the board.

'The buffet-car attendant – bags of means, but no motive.' He looked round with a raised eyebrow. There was no dissent and he put a line through her name.

'Sophie Gough? She knew Brett, but she dumped him and deleted him from her Friends Inc account. She was working in her office all day, and there are multiple clients as witness to that. No way she could have been on the train. No motive and no means.'

'Mrs Wallace – she's turned up on at least two occasions we know of, to argue with Wallace about money and to disrupt his dates. She was also stalking him through a fraudulent Friends Inc account. But she has an alibi for that day, as she was at work. Has anyone checked that alibi?' he interrupted himself.

'I'll give the estate agents a ring,' said Chris, making a note.

'Frances Lyell – she also claims to have dumped Wallace because of Mrs Wallace but, unlike Sophie Gough, she didn't delete him from her account. She was on the train, the app would have told her he was also on the train, but she claims they weren't on speaking terms and that she didn't go to the buffet car. Any comments anyone?'

Chris caught his eye. 'I'll check with the Kings Arms, to get their perspective on the public row.'

Jill chipped in, 'I can't find anything on the CCTV that shows her going to the buffet car at any time. That red hat is very eye-catching, so it was easy to check.'

Greg paused at the whiteboard, struck by a sudden thought. 'That may have been precisely the point. Jill, take another look, but from the opposite perspective. Don't look for the red hat. Check to see if she ever left her seat, then check who moved into or out of the buffet car during that time period.

'Finally, we need to do more work on the oldest motive of all. Who benefits? We know he recently changed his will so that his wife did not benefit, and other relatives did. Did his wife know? Did the new beneficiaries know? We need a chat with the solicitor who drew up the will.'

'Who works in the same company as the two lawyers who were on the train,' Chris reminded him.

'So she does.' As he spoke, his phone buzzed, and he glanced at the screen. 'It's Ned,' he said, then waited in silence. When he rang off, he looked round the room. 'It was cyanide,' he said. 'No traces found in any of the samples taken from the train passengers, but there were traces in two of those mini milk cartons. As we know, they found Wallace's phone in the toilet at the end of Coach B. They've also found a plastic bag and a blonde wig in the waste tank serving the first-class compartments. Jill, add blonde hair to your list of targets on the CCTV.

'Chris, you and I will go to see the solicitor, Fiona Harrison. Bill, can you do the checking on the wife's alibi? And have a word with Friends Inc while you're at it. See if there's any way the wife could have found out about his dates through their database.'

***

Fiona was young, black haired, newly qualified and keen to help. She eagerly laid out all the paperwork connected with Brett Wallace's will on the conference room table. 'I've never been involved with anything like this,' she enthused. Chris noted that her enthusiasm seemed as much for the detective as the circumstances and was surprised how jealous that made her feel.

Still batting black eyelashes at Greg, Fiona gushed, 'It's all here. I think you've had the gist already, but essentially it was a straightforward will. The only complication was the removal of his wife as a beneficiary, which I pointed out might be challengeable, but we added a side letter explaining that she'd already received the family home as part of their separation agreement and couldn't reasonably expect any more in the circumstances.'

'Was there anything about the circumstances that was unusual?' asked Greg.

'Well, a little, I suppose, in that when there's an abusive partner it's usually the woman who is the victim.'

'But not in this case?'

'No. Not in this case.'

'Was the abuse physical?' asked Chris, feeling the need to make it clear she was still in the room.

'I believe so, on occasion,' replied Fiona, addressing her answer to Greg. 'I realise that might seem hard to believe, but I think he was inhibited from retaliating by being a gentleman. Or at least, he had been brought up to think that hitting women was the absolute end. But I also got the impression a lot of the abuse was emotional. It seemed he could never do anything on his own or for himself, without her throwing a tantrum. He never got to see his family and never went out with friends because, if he did, the payback when he got home just wasn't worth it. He told me, once, that he'd gone to see his mother before she died, and when he got home, his wife was cutting his books into shreds "as a punishment for withdrawing his attention from her".'

'But you're quoting his version, aren't you?' asked Chris. 'Did you see anything yourself that would support his claims?'

'I had a letter from her,' said Fiona with a touch of indignation. 'After I let her know formally about the change in the will, I got a reply accusing me of influencing the outcome for my own reasons and to my own benefit.'

'Did you keep a copy?' said Chris.

'Of course. I'll forward it to you.'

'But you didn't benefit from the will, did you?' asked Greg.

'Of course not. That would be totally improper. You've seen it. The money goes to family and a bit to charities. We've contacted everyone now, so they all know the outcome.'

‘Do you know Ms Hendry?’ asked Chris somewhat abruptly.

‘Only by sight,’ replied Fiona. ‘This is a big company, and she’s a partner.’

‘And her assistant, Richard Wentworth?’

‘I know him better. We go to the same gym, and we have a coffee together occasionally.’

‘Have you discussed the Wallace will with either of them?’ asked Greg.

‘No, never,’ she said, but she hesitated.

‘Are you sure?’ said Chris.

‘I might have mentioned a bonkers wife, but that’s all. None of the detail of the will.’

As Greg and Chris were leaving, Fiona caught Greg by the sleeve. ‘I go to the gym in Thorpe St Andrew,’ she said, ‘if you’re ever passing let me know. It’s a good gym and they do great coffee.’

Greg, to his considerable embarrassment, didn’t know what to say, and stuttered something like ‘thank you’, under the exceedingly sardonic eye being bent upon him by Chris.

‘Unbelievable,’ she said as they got into the car, every syllable getting its due weight. ‘Your irresistible attraction strikes again.’ Feeling that whatever he said would be wrong on so many fronts, Greg opted to say nothing. He was saved by Chris’s phone ringing. By the time she rang off, her mind was on other things.

‘That was the Kings Arms,’ she said. ‘According to the waitress who was serving Wallace and Frances Lyell, it was

Wallace who did the dumping and Lyell who didn't take it well.'

'Is she sure? How much of the conversation was she able to hear?' asked Greg sceptically.

'She didn't hear much of the conversation. Just Wallace saying he was sorry it wasn't working, then she had to clear the dishes. But when she came back with the dessert menu, I think agog to hear the next instalment, she was just in time to see Lyell tip a nearly full pint of beer over his head, and stalk off saying something like "he'd be sorry".'

'Well now,' began Greg, but was interrupted by his own phone ringing. As Greg answered it on the hands-free while manoeuvring into traffic, they were both deafened by an excited bellow from Bill. 'Say that again,' said Greg, 'and not so loud this time.'

'Mrs Wallace,' he said, this time moderating the volume to something approaching a mere shout. 'Her alibi doesn't check. She wasn't in the office, she was with clients, and two of the clients say she didn't turn up. She could have been anywhere.'

'She could have been on the train.' Greg finished the sentence for him. 'We need to check that out. What about Friends Inc?'

'They're still maintaining their security is impregnable, but I'm calling round there now to see if they've turned anything up.' Bill rang off, leaving a ringing silence behind him.

'Our Ms Lyell is looking interesting, and so is Mrs Wallace. We seem to have gone from no suspects to a surplus,' remarked Greg. 'Let's take a closer look at both.'

***

They had scarcely turned in at the Wymondham HQ car park when the phone rang again.

'I have something to show you,' said Jill's voice. A swift walk through the corridors brought them to the operations room and Jill's array of three screens. She wasn't there. Greg looked round the room, but it seemed not being there was a popular choice.

'I wasn't that bad this morning, was I?' he asked.

'Not much worse than normal,' was Chris's unpromising reply. 'Roughly on a par with "that driver in front is an idiot" but a long way short of "have we really run out of coffee".' She was interrupted by a buzz from her phone and, to Greg's relief, turned aside to take the call. By the time she rang off, Jill was back and rushing to her desk.

'Sorry,' she said. 'Had to just pop out for a moment. Here, this is what I wanted to show you.' She tapped away on her keyboard for a moment, then the screen in the centre of the display produced a fuzzy image of a train carriage. Watching carefully, they saw a woman in a red cap stand up from her seat and head to the back of the carriage.

'Note the time, said Jill.' As they continued to watch, a blonde woman in a blue coverall came down the centre aisle and passed under the camera.

'Is that the buffet-car attendant? asked Chris. 'Janice what's-her-name?'

'It could be, couldn't it,' said Jill. 'But I don't think so. Look at what shows up on the camera in the buffet car about four minutes later.'

She tapped again. The image on the centre screen froze, and the screen to the left showed the interior of the buffet car. In the background, one woman in a coverall seemed to be setting up a trolley. In the foreground, a second woman, similarly dressed, was already heading down the first-class carriages, a small basket in her hand.

'I think that is our perp,' said Jill, 'handing out milk and sugar. The cyanide must have already been in the milk cartons.'

'But why didn't Janice see the stranger messing about in the buffet car?' said Greg.

'Well, she definitely had her back to the blonde,' said Jill.

'And the guard said she was in the habit of wearing headphones while she was setting up,' said Chris. 'That would have meant she couldn't hear anything going on behind her.'

'That's what they are!' said Jill. 'Of course. I could see something on the video, but it wasn't very clear. Headphones make sense. But I said, note the time. Now let's go back to the camera in Coach B.' She restarted the video on the centre screen. As they watched, they saw a blonde woman go back to the end of the carriage, then shortly after, the woman in the red cap returned to her seat.

'Oh boy,' said Chris. 'So, Frances Lyell left her seat, and while she was somewhere else, a blonde woman in an overall went down to the buffet car and apparently left milk and sugar sachets in coaches C and B. Did she go into Coach A?'

'Yes. And seems to have left milk and sugar there too. Then disappeared off-screen.'

'Your theory being?' said Chris.

'That Frances Lyell went into the loo, removed her red cap, replaced it with a blonde wig and put an overall on, before going down to the buffet car and then handing out milk etc throughout First Class. Then returned to the loo, removed the wig and dumped it, replaced her red cap and went back to her seat.'

'But why go into the buffet car at all? Surely doing that risked her being spotted by Janice. She couldn't have known that Janice would be listening to Robbie Williams on headphones,' said Greg.

'My guess is, that with the cyanide in the milk cartons, she only had just a couple of doctored cartons to leave on Brett Wallace's table. She can't have had many, because you don't see her carrying anything much until she picks up the basket in the buffet. I think she needed the normal supply to provide cover while she wandered down First Class pretending to be a normal attendant.'

There was a pause, then Chris said, 'Damn good job I drink my coffee black.' There was another pause while Greg took that in.

'You mean,' he said slowly, 'she didn't care much if there was any collateral damage.'

'Quite. Anyone else in an adjacent seat could easily have used a doctored carton too.'

Greg shuddered slightly, then added, 'But of course, this is all circumstantial and supposition. Well done, Jill, I think this is a very promising lead. But we need evidence.'

'Ah, that reminds me,' said Chris. 'That was Bill on the phone just now. He's at Friends Inc with a very mortified Mr Nesbitt. It seems their security systems were more than a little lacking.'

'In what way?' asked Greg. 'I thought he was a computer whizzkid!'

'He was. Is! There's nothing wrong with their software security. But he's not such a whizz when it comes to people. Their firewalls are pretty impregnable to hacking, but they're very vulnerable to good old-fashioned theft. They have a junior in the office who reckoned she wasn't being paid enough and succumbed to temptation.'

'Which particular temptation?' asked Greg.

'A bribe from a "mistreated wife" or in other words, Mrs Wallace. It seems Mrs Wallace has been paying for information on her ex-husband's dates.'

7

That evening

It had been a long day, and showed no signs of being over for anyone, any time soon. Jill was still immersed in videos. Bill was showing distinct signs of exasperation as he strove to get past the Met's righteous indignation at being found wanting, in order to get any evidence of where Mrs Wallace had spent the day in question. The Friends Inc office junior, lips plumped to the point of deformity, and make-up so excessive as to give the appearance of enamelling, was in turns aggressively self-justifying and tearfully whinging. Chris gave the girl's overweening sense of entitlement short shrift and informed her that she was looking at a criminal record unless her employers were feeling excessively generous. She knew already that Frankie was in no rush to press charges because of the risk of negative publicity but saw no harm in handing out a crime-preventative fright.

'I din't see no harm in it,' the girl whined. 'E 'ad walked out on 'er after all. 'E owed 'er, din't 'e?'

'Never mind that,' said Chris. 'Just explain to me what your arrangement was.'

'Wot?' said the girl, confused.

'I mean,' said Chris – wondering first, if it was possible to use words of less than one syllable, and second, how on earth the girl had got the job in the first place – 'how did you contact Mrs Wallace?'

'She rang me. Nearly every day.'

'And you told her what?'

'When 'e was meeting someone, and where.'

'And how did you get paid?'

'She put money into my bank account.'

'Excellent,' said Chris. 'In that case, I'd like copies of your bank statements, please.'

Dashing into Greg's office, waving a sheaf of printouts at him, she paused and sat down as she realised he was busy with Jill.

'The facial recognition software was really helpful for screening the train passengers and the attendees at the NHS conference,' she was saying. 'I was looking for Mrs Wallace, but on the spur of the moment I tried one or two other images as well. I got nothing on Mrs W, but I did find Ms Lyell. At the conference.'

'Did you indeed?' said Greg. 'That's very interesting. Well done again, Jill. So, no sign of Mrs Wallace amongst the train passengers but, despite her protestations, Frances Lyell did not spend her day in London seeing the sights. She attended the same NHS conference Brett Wallace was at. That looks like stalking to me.

'Chris, did you have something as well?'

'Clear evidence that Mrs Wallace was paying for information on her husband's dating arrangements, but no evidence she knew he was in London that day. The payments into Jodi Teller's account match the dates when Brett Wallace had arranged to meet up with another Friends Inc client. But as the London trip was work, not social, clearly Jodi didn't know about it and therefore neither did Mrs Wallace. Whatever she was up to when she missed seeing her clients that day, we have no evidence she was chasing her husband around, nor that she was on that train.'

'While it does look very much like Frances Lyell was stalking him. Let's pay her a visit. She'll be home by now.'

It was after nine o'clock by the time they pulled up outside the small, detached cottage that was Frances Lyell's Reedham home.

'At least it's on our way home,' said Chris, hoping for bed before midnight at least.

'Not if we arrest her,' said Greg, reading her mind. 'So don't hold your breath for an early night.'

There were lights showing in the hall and front room. Despite that, banging on the front door produced nothing but a volley of nervous barking. Greg tried again, and for a third time, before getting any response. Eventually, Frances Lyell stuck her head out of the narrow gap permitted by a door still on a chain.

'Yes,' she snapped. 'What now?'

'We have some further questions to ask you,' said Greg.

'Now?' she asked. 'At this hour?'

'Yes, now,' he said firmly. 'We can do it here, or you can accompany us to the station. Your choice.'

'Oh, very well,' she said and opened the door.

'Wait in there,' she said, indicating the front room. 'I'll be with you in a moment.'

The room was already occupied by the barking dog. 'Shut it,' snapped Lyell, presumably to the dog, and leaving the three of them together, she pulled the door to behind her.

Greg and Chris regarded the dog with suspicion. The dog returned the favour but stopped barking. One wary eye on their canine companion, Greg sat down on an armchair by the gas fire. Chris opted for a Windsor chair near the door.

'Now what?' Chris asked. The room smelled slightly of dog, and strongly of curry. Presumably the olfactory remnants of Ms Lyell's supper.

'Well at least it's stopped barking,' said Greg, and held out a hand to the dog. This provoked a volley of more barking, which only gradually subsided. Resisting the temptation to snatch his hand away, Greg continued to hold it out and eventually the dog, which looked like a boxer cross, ventured close enough to take a sniff, then backed off again. Chris shuffled in her hard chair, the dog whipped round to glare at her, then went back to Greg's hand.

'Come on, old girl,' said Greg. 'I'm harmless you know. Sorry I haven't anything to give you. You look a bit hungry.'

'That's not very reassuring,' said Chris, not a great lover of large, hungry dogs. Greg was by now almost crooning to the dog, which had approached closely enough to have its flank stroked. Greg stiffened, dared to lift one of the dog's ears for a closer look then, as the dog jerked sideways, he reverted to stroking it.

'That's a cigarette burn,' he said to Chris in a conversational tone.

'It's what?' asked Chris. 'Are you sure?'

'Shush, don't sound so excited,' replied Greg. 'You'll set the dog off again. I'm sure, I've seen it before. This dog's been burned with cigarette ends.'

'I wonder if it's Lyell or someone else?' asked Chris.

'That's the interesting question. But some of the burns look recent.'

'Some of them! How many are there?' Chris was horrified.

'At least four. I can't see the other side, so probably more. I don't think I like our Ms Lyell,' said Greg. 'Come to that, she's been gone a long time. Where is she?'

'I'll check,' said Chris. Moving slowly, to avoid disturbing the dog, she opened the door and went into the hall. Greg heard her moving around and calling Ms Lyell, but stayed where he was, with the dog. Chris was back in moments.

'Legged it,' she said succinctly. 'Her car's gone. At least, the one that was by the garage when we came in isn't there any more.'

'Has she indeed,' said Greg. 'That's very interesting. Okay. Get uniform here and Ned's team. We don't need a warrant. She invited us in. Get an APB out for her car, the RSPCA for this dog, then let's go home for some sleep.'

***

Greg's hope for sleep was also doomed to disappointment. Almost an hour had passed by the time a couple of constables and a SOCO turned up to take over at the Lyell address. A van from the dog pound followed, and the dog was taken into what Greg termed protective custody after the SOCO, a slim dark woman that Greg vaguely recognised, took photographs of its head and ears. She agreed with Greg's diagnosis of the round burn marks.

The dog safely carried away, the dark woman pounced with satisfaction on a laptop.

'I'm sorry,' said Greg to the back of her head. 'I'm sure we've met before, but I don't know your name.'

'We have,' she said, turning her head from the laptop. 'On the clifftop near Bacton when I found some evidence stuck in the bushes. I'm Gerry Dane.'

'I remember,' said Greg. 'Good to see you again. I assume you're taking the laptop in for analysis.' He was slightly concerned about data being lost as a result of inexpert examination, and his concern was transparent to Gerry.

'Of course,' she said. 'But I'll have a quick look first, for anything obvious. If you're worried,' she added, 'don't be.

It'll probably be me who does the later examination as well. I do know what I'm doing.'

Greg nodded. 'Thank you,' he said, and turned to the uniformed colleagues searching the property. The small house yielded nothing of obvious interest, but the garden shed was different. Surveying the pile of ageing garden tools and empty plastic plant pots, Greg concluded that Ms Lyell was not an enthusiastic gardener.

'That's not what I wanted to show you, sir,' said the constable who had conducted the search.

'You are?' asked Greg.

'Constable Den Barnes,' he replied. 'This is what I thought you ought to see.' He shone his torch on the back wall of the shed, where it butted up to the house. Incongruous amongst the rusty tools was a steel gun cabinet, apparently bolted through the wooden shed wall and into the side of the house. It was standing open and held nothing except an empty box that appeared to have contained shotgun cartridges, a tin and small glass vial. 'The glass bottle says "strychnine" and the tin contains Cymag gassing powder,' said Constable Barnes.

'No sign of a shotgun?' asked Greg.

'No.'

Emerging from the garden shed into the spatter of a rain shower, Greg headed to his car, and the radio.

'That APB,' he said to the despatcher. 'Add a warning: *Believed armed. Do not approach.*'

'Roger,' said the voice.

'Any news on our quarry?' Greg added.

'Not yet.'

At that point he was distracted by Chris waving from the house. 'Gerry's got something from the laptop,' she said.

Greg returned up the path, the rain getting harder, dodged a constable carrying a box out of the house and rejoined Gerry in the kitchen.

'Hi,' she said. 'I've got into the laptop. It was easy. Like a lot of people, she had a list of passwords in a folder hidden in her bookcase. And I think you need to see something.'

The laptop was open on the kitchen table, showing a stream of personal photos obviously used as a screen save. 'This,' said Gerry, interrupting the screen save. 'This is in her browsing history.'

It was a piece of video from the dark web, showing the gruesome outcome of an American school mass shooting. 'It's not the only one,' she added. 'I've found at least eight similar bits of footage in just the last fifteen minutes. And there's something else I haven't been able to open. It looks like a piece of video, but it's password-protected. I need to do some more work on that.'

***

Reporting to his chief superintendent, Margaret Tayler, by phone, Greg wound up with 'I've put out a *Do not Approach* warning. It may be OTT but I'm afraid not. We've good reason to believe she's already killed once, with few precautions, if any, to protect bystanders. And her internet browsing history is disturbing to say the least. I don't like how she's treated the dog either. In fact, the more I learn about Lyell, the less there is to like.'

'I agree,' said Margaret. 'Assuming it was her that burned the dog. But I've seen the report from Gerry Dane. That alone is worrying. Do we have any better idea what she's armed with? I've put the armed response team on standby and they're asking for more details.'

'A shotgun is probable, given the empty ammo box. We're still making enquiries and forensics are doing more checks on her laptop, but at the moment we know no more than that.

'Could you hold on please, boss, I've got a message coming through, flagged as urgent.'

A pause, and then Greg said, 'Her phone's been turned on long enough for triangulation. When it pinged, she was between Norwich City football ground and the railway station. I'm on my way.'

8

Showdown

A mad dash down the A47 with blue lights flashing, saw Greg taking the roundabout near County Hall only twenty minutes later.

'That must be a record,' he said, concentrating grimly on the road ahead and the, fortunately few, drivers who were slow to get out of his way. He sped on, down toward the football ground, and Chris picked up the radio as an incomprehensible squawk made itself apparent.

'Say again,' she said.

'Shots fired in the railway station. Casualties reported. Major incident declared.'

'Got it,' said Chris. 'We're about three minutes out. Where should we rendezvous?'

'Station forecourt,' said despatch. 'Station is locked down and uniformed officers are deploying along the tracks. All incoming trains halted. Armed response are also on their way.'

In the few minutes it took to arrive at the station approaches, police cars had blocked access. Pulling across the carriageway, and incidentally blocking it to traffic in every direction, Greg stuck his head out and waved his warrant card. The officer on duty recognised him and waved him through just before a late-evening road-rage riot broke out behind him. Greg pulled straight up to the entrance portico and leaped out, looking round for the officer in charge. Chris, not far behind him, grabbed stab vests from the back seat and handed him one.

'Better than nothing,' she said. With relief, Greg recognised Jim Henning in the centre of a knot of officers. As he walked briskly toward them, the heavens reopened with a major downpour and the first media van turned up at the traffic barrier, only to be turned away.

They splashed through the already forming puddles and took shelter with the clump of other officers under the portico. Even as they approached, four dark-clad figures equipped with night scopes and carbines peeled off and headed into the station at a trot. As they did so, the station lights abruptly went out, plunging the scene into darkness.

'What's the situation?' asked Greg.

Jim turned to him. 'Lyell is on Platform 2. Roughly thirty metres down and apparently lying behind a pillar and a cleaning trolley. The train was the 9 pm from Liverpool Street. It seems she dumped her car in the car park without actually bothering to park it in a bay, ran in past the customer-service office and straight onto the platform just as the train pulled in. According to staff, she was moving fast, and by the time anyone realised she was armed, she had reached the platform. When the passengers started to detrain, she opened fire. There are at least three casualties on the platform that we can see and maybe more on the train. A few younger passengers were lucky enough, and fast enough, to make it to the exit barriers and jump over them. They took cover in the shop. One of them says Lyell tried to rush into the train, but someone, guard or driver, had the good sense to close the doors. Presumably they were alerted by the noise. A shotgun going off in that space must have sounded like a cannon! There are some reports she fired at the train windows, but, since I got here, she's been holed up behind that cleaning trolley.'

Greg turned to a man in a flak jacket bearing 'Inspector' insignia with the name 'Jones' and recognised the firearms team leader from a hostage situation in Fleggburgh a few months before.

'What next?' he asked, but was interrupted by a small but forceful paramedic.

'There are casualties we need to get to,' she said. 'They need our help now. It may be too late for some, but—'

'Yes, I understand,' said Inspector Jones but until we've neutralised the threat, you go no closer. Understand?'

She nodded impatiently but took a short step back and reported on her radio in an undertone.

'Anyone tried talking to Lyell?' asked Greg.

'Not yet. And no one's going anywhere near her until I have marksmen in position. I have one climbing onto the roof of the toilet block, and a couple trying to get close enough along the tracks. Until they're in place, no one leaves this entrance hall. Understood?'

'And if she rushes this way?' asked Greg.

'Then I have three men in place behind the platform barriers, with night scopes. With the lights out, the advantage is with us. We can see her and, unless she's similarly equipped, and we don't think she is, she can't see us. If she makes a threatening move, they'll take her down. She's not getting off that platform except in handcuffs or on a stretcher. The lights will go back up when my marksmen are in place, and with luck we'll get her then.'

'Armament?' asked Greg.

Jim replied, 'Over-and-under shotgun and what seems to be a pump-action shotgun. That's all, so far as we know. But, unfortunately, she's had plenty of time to reload.'

A silence fell, broken by the rattle of rain on the station roof, the muffled sound of engines in the car park outside and the distant tolling of a bell from the cathedral.

Inspector Jones turned to his radio; there was a brief exchange as the marksmen reported their readiness, then the lights came back on with a suddenness that made Greg blink. There were shouts from the platform, and then more shouting from a female voice. Moving cautiously but swiftly, Greg scrambled across the concourse in the cover provided by the customer-service office, then slid round the side of the office until he could see down the platform. Not entirely to his surprise, he felt Chris at his elbow.

The train was silent, its doors closed and no lights on. Greg assumed the driver had extinguished those and turned his attention to a tall shape in a black coat moving toward the end of the platform, brandishing a shotgun in her right hand. The second gun seemed to be lying on the ground some paces behind her. The radio muttered again, and Greg was close enough to hear the marksman on the roof of the toilet block indicate that he had the target and ask for permission to shoot.

Inspector Jones replied into the radio, 'You know what to do,' then shouted in a loud voice, 'ARMED POLICE! DROP YOUR WEAPONS! DROP YOUR WEAPONS!'

The shape kept walking and a laser spot appeared on the chest of the black coat just as she threw something down the platform. A can bounced and rolled toward the entrance barriers. Greg recognised it as the twin of the can he had seen in Lyell's gun cabinet, but his shout of 'Cyanide! It's Cymag!' was drowned in the blast of the shotgun and the simultaneous crack of the marksman's carbine.

The black figure flew backward, then lay still. The can, hit by many shotgun pellets, spun round, then bounced over the edge of the platform onto the tracks, shedding a white powder as it went. There was a rush toward the platform, but Greg threw himself in front of the array of police and paramedics, his arms outstretched to stop them.

'That tin was Cymag. Cyanide gassing powder,' he shouted. 'Keep everyone back.'

'Hose it away,' suggested someone. Both Jim and Chris said, 'No!' explosively.

'It emits the gas when it gets wet,' said Chris.

'But it's heavier than air,' added Jim. They peered at the can and powder on the tracks below platform level.

Greg was on his phone, taking advice from Margaret. 'Okay,' he said. 'Paramedics can go in wearing breathing kits to recover the casualties. The fire brigade can supply extra sets. Everyone else stays on the train or outside the station until the cleanup squad has been in and swept it up.'

'What about Lyell?'

'We go and get her as well. Also with breathing kits. It's not worth taking risks now. She's going nowhere.'

9

Aftermath

Equipped with Fire Service supplied breathing kits, Greg and Jim went forward together with Inspector Jones, a paramedic and a marksman; the latter still armed and alert. As they approached Lyell, a bustle behind them signalled the arrival of the cleanup squad. Frances Lyell was lying on her back, arms outstretched, just had she had fallen. Jones put out a hand as the paramedic showed signs of rushing in and, watched closely by his marksman, checked for vital signs. Greg thought that, from where he was standing, the hole in her chest and the blood which had flowed onto the platform beneath her were diagnostic enough. Jones stood up, shaking his head, then nodded to the paramedic, who stepped forward, checked for carotid and radial pulse, and stood up, also shaking her head. The marksman made his weapon safe and, at a nod from Jones, headed back to the station entrance.

Greg stepped forward but was waved back again.

'We'll just wait for the dog,' said Jones. 'It's not going to make any difference to her now, and I'd sooner we checked for explosives before we move her.'

'I don't think she had time,' said Greg. 'She left the house in a hurry while we were there. There's been no suggestion of explosives at her property other than those in shotgun cartridges. This was a fairly low-tech event.'

'Nonetheless,' said Jones unmoved, 'we'll go by the book. Fine idiot I'd look if she had an explosive vest, and you went into orbit over Norwich.'

The clatter of claws and a loud panting advertised the arrival of Turbo, springer spaniel sniffer dog and one of Greg's favourite staff members. Keeping him well clear of the cleanup squad currently engaged in hoovering up cyanide gassing powder from the railway tracks, Jenny, his chauffeur – or handler, depending on your point of view – brought him over to the body, in which he showed very little interest.

'Clear,' said Jenny, and whisked Turbo away before he could come to harm.

The train doors opened to allow the paramedics not already busy with the other bodies on the platform to board. Greg knelt by Lyell's body, carefully keeping his trouser knees out of the spilled blood, and checked her pockets. Apart from a couple of tissues, all he turned up was a memory stick. He dropped it into an evidence bag held out by Chris and got to his feet.

'Let's get the mortuary team,' he said. 'Do we have a casualty list?'

'Numbers, yes, but not a complete list of names,' said Chris, who'd been keeping in touch with the paramedic in overall charge. 'Of the three on the platform, two are dead and one has life-changing injuries but may survive. Of those on the train, only one is seriously hurt. There are five who will be taken to hospital to have shotgun pellets removed. Four more, including a member of the train crew, have cuts and bruises as a result of being trampled in the rush to get back on the train, and there's one possible heart attack caused by the general panic. It could have been a lot worse.'

The sound of ambulance sirens rose in the air as the first of the seriously injured were taken away, and Greg turned to look at Jones. 'We'll all need to make detailed reports,' he said. 'And sooner is always best. The inquest on Frances Lyell will be looking at the question of lawful or unlawful killing.'

'Yes, sir,' said Jones, and strode away to rejoin his men.

Greg looked at Jim, then Chris. 'And the inquests on the rest of tonight's casualties will be looking at what more I could have done to prevent this disaster,' he said. His face was bleak.

Chris opened her mouth to speak, then shut it again at a glance from Jim. 'Best we write our reports in the morning,' he said. 'It's too late now. And time will give us a better perspective.'

'Maybe,' said Greg, unconvinced, and took up his phone to update Margaret. Then, on her orders, he handed over to the senior uniformed officer present to manage the scene, collected Chris from where she was supervising the removal of evidence bags, and headed for home.

By the time they reached Greg's cottage on the banks of the Bure, both Greg and Chris were simultaneously wired and knackered. In unspoken agreement they both took a few minutes to jot down key reactions to the evening's events, interrupted only by Bobby's assertions that she was starving and neglected.

'Take no notice,' said Greg over his shoulder. 'Her automatic cat feeder has been on. She has eaten. She's just trying it on.' He sighed and leaned back in his chair at the kitchen table. 'I'm ready for bed,' he added, 'but I must admit I'm going to struggle to sleep.'

'Chamomile tea,' said Chris decisively.

'Tastes like silage,' complained Greg.

'That's what you always say. And by the time you've finished adding sugar, I imagine it tastes like silage that's overheated and caramelised,' replied Chris. 'But it does help.'

Greg looked across the kitchen and noted that she too was reeling with tiredness. 'I'll bring it up,' he said, taking the kettle from her hand. 'Go on. I'll be up in a minute.'

***

The morning brought light, more rain, and a message to call at the mortuary on his way in to work. Greg stood in his conservatory, enjoying the sight of raindrops pattering the smooth surface of the river, then turned away to tip the final dregs of his morning coffee into the sink and put his mug in the dishwasher.

'Chris,' he hollered up the stairs. 'Step on it, we're due at the mortuary.' A clatter of footsteps on stairs announced her arrival at ground level, wearing a black skirt, yellow and pink patterned jumper and vivid blue scarf.

'Well,' said Greg, surveying the vision currently blasting colour into every corner of his normally dark hall. 'That's, erm, eye-catching. However, is it entirely, erm, appropriate for a mortuary?'

'I don't think the occupants are going to object any time soon,' she remarked just a little tartly. 'But in any event, I'm not going to the mortuary.'

'You're not?'

'No. Not unless it's a big deal. I thought my time would be better spent with our friend Gerry and the video file she was trying to get into.'

'The memory stick we took off Lyell's body last night should have reached her by now. I want to know what's on that as well,' said Greg.

'Sure,' said Chris, landed a quick kiss on his cheek and turned away. 'Look after yourself,' she added over her shoulder, and got into her little Ka.

***

By the time Greg arrived at the mortuary, Dr Paisley was gloved, gowned and dictating the beginning of her report as she reviewed the external appearance of what remained of Frances Lyell. The body lay naked and supine on the steel table, the single bullet wound to the chest the only sign of damage.

'Female, forty-two years old, apparently in good physical condition and average weight,' dictated Dr Paisley. Greg hovered in the vicinity of the feet, noting that Lyell had rather beautiful feet, with high arches and straight toes. The toenails were varnished a pale pink to match those on her fingers. Dr Paisley made the long central incision and peeled back the skin layers, with particular attention to the chest cavity. All Greg could see, from his vantage point, was a mess of purplish blood obscuring the details of the thoracic organs. Dr Paisley's elegant long neck bent over her work, there was a pause, and she produced with a sigh of triumph a 9 mm bullet, which she dropped with a clatter into a small dish.

'I gather there was just one shot,' she said.

'That's right,' said Greg. 'From a marksman on the roof of the toilet block.'

'How far off was he, would you say?' asked Dr Paisley.

'Roughly eighty to a hundred metres, I would think.'

'Then, depending on your perspective, it was a good shot,' she said. 'That's close to the limit of accuracy for a carbine, and the bullet went straight through the aorta. She would have bled out in seconds.'

'I don't think he was necessarily aiming for lethality,' said Greg. 'I believe his orders were to stop her, and a chest shot has the best chance of doing that.'

'I'm not arguing,' said the doctor drily. 'I have two more post-mortems this morning from the incident – both her victims. I'm just saying that, at that distance, she might have regarded herself as unlucky.'

'Any other findings relevant to the inquest?' asked Greg.

'Not that I've seen so far, and, frankly, I don't expect to find any. You'll need to look elsewhere for an explanation of why an apparently normal civil servant suddenly poisons a boyfriend and then goes on the rampage at Norwich Railway Station.'

'What should I be looking for, doc?' asked Greg. 'I'm feeling there should have been something in her manner that tipped me off. Something that I could have picked up on that might have prevented this. If I'd arrested her when I arrived at her house, there'd be people alive today instead of lying on your tables, and more who wouldn't be in hospital with life-changing injuries.'

Dr Paisley stripped her gloves off and turned round. 'You're feeling responsible,' she said.

'You bet I am. And the inevitable investigation will be looking to see if I am. So I really could do with knowing, did I miss something? Was it my fault?'

'No way,' said the doctor firmly. 'I'm sure this will have been said to you before, but it's nonetheless true. The responsibility lies with the person who fired the shotguns, no one else. As to whether you could have predicted her actions, was there anything at all that suggested she might flip or, indeed, that she was armed to do so?'

'Nothing,' said Greg, perching on a stool. 'I was sure she was stalking the train murder victim, and that had moved her sharply up the list of likely suspects for his murder, but I had no definitive proof she killed him. It was just about possible there was another explanation for what looked like her movements on the train that day. I still don't have that proof, for that matter. Although it's hard to see why she reacted as she did if she wasn't involved in murdering Brett Wallace.'

***

Back in Wymondham, Greg was pleasantly surprised to get through the door without being greeted by a command to see the Chief Super asap. Dumping phone and car keys on his desk, he went hunting for colleagues and coffee, not necessarily in that order. Large mug of strong black in hand, he poked his head round a few doors to find Jim, Bill and Jill all keen to pass on information.

'Hold on, hold on,' he said. 'Let's do this in some sort of order.' He was interrupted by Chris galloping down the corridor, her face a good match for the brighter elements of her jumper.

'Something you really need to see,' she said, waving, and almost dropping, her battered iPad.

'This way,' said Greg, pointing into the ops room, where he took up his usual stance by the whiteboard. 'I think you've all got updates for me and I'm eager to hear them,' he said. 'But bear with me just a moment. I'm feeling the need for some sort of logical order in this case. At the moment it feels a bit of a muddle, and that's my fault not yours. Events have overtaken us, and I'd like to pre-empt the inevitable demand from upstairs for a coherent narrative. So!

'First of all, what do we know? Brett Wallace died three days ago on the Norwich Express from Liverpool Street, as a result of cyanide poisoning. The cyanide was administered through the milk he put in his railway coffee.

'Brett Wallace had been arranging dates online through the Friends Inc website. At least one of his recent dates had dumped him when his estranged wife turned up and made a fuss. His wife had been stalking him by getting information from a Friends Inc employee on when and where he was meeting women.

'Frances Lyell had at least three dates with Wallace but was dumped by him a week ago. We have supporting testimony to that effect from a waitress at the Kings Arms. We had at least two possible stalkers for Wallace: his estranged wife and Lyell. The latter definitely turned up at an NHS conference in which she had no professional interest, as confirmed by CCTV, and then later followed him onto that train. As for his wife, we know she missed appointments that day, but we can't find her on CCTV either at the conference or on the train. Yes, Bill?' said Greg in response to an arm waving about.

'The latest on the wife,' said Bill, flipping through his notebook. 'When she should have been seeing clients, she was visiting building societies in Victoria Street, trying to remortgage the Muswell Hill house. She admitted as much to me over the phone, in exchange for me not shopping her to her employer. I checked with a couple of the building societies and her alibi is good.'

'Well done, Bill,' said Greg. 'Pity the chaps from the Met weren't as thorough. We can cross her off then,' he added, and put a line through her name on the whiteboard. 'Back to Frances Lyell. We know from CCTV that a woman of her height and general shape but with blonde hair left milk cartons at Brett Wallace's seat, and CCTV also shows that between those times Lyell was absent from her seat in Coach B. A blonde wig was found in the drains at the end of the train.'

Jill piped up. 'Forensics have found her DNA on the wig,' she said. 'Latest report says they found hair follicles inside the wig, that came from Lyell.'

'Good. Thanks, Jill,' said Greg and added a tick to the whiteboard. 'Chris and I went to Lyell's home last night to follow up on the info about her attending the NHS conference. She invited us in, then left us with her dog.'

'Which had cigarette burns on its ears,' interrupted Chris. 'Poor thing.'

'While we were waiting in her living room,' went on Greg, 'she got in her car and drove off. When we searched her house, it became clear she was probably armed, and as it transpired, she'd taken two shotguns and a canister of cyanide gassing powder with her. She drove to Norwich Railway Station and embarked on a killing spree before being taken down herself by a police marksman.

'Questions that leap to mind include:

'Where did she get the cyanide and, for that matter, the vial of strychnine that was also found at her home?

'What sparked the original murder?

'And what set off the killing spree?'

'And, where did she get the cyanide she used to poison Wallace?' added Jim.

'Wouldn't that have been the same stuff as in the tin?' asked Greg.

'No, can't have been,' said Jim. 'Cymag is a powder that emits cyanide gas when it comes into contact with water. It couldn't have been in the milk. The cyanide in the milk has to have been a solid.'

Greg made another note. 'Good point,' he said. 'So she's accessed at least three distinct forms of poison, none of which are currently available to the public.'

'That's right,' said Chris. 'Both strychnine and Cymag used to be used on farms, but they've been withdrawn for some years. But she did work for Defra. Perhaps she came across them on a farm somewhere. But that doesn't explain the cyanide salt.'

'When you came in, you said you had something to show us,' said Greg. 'What was it?'

'Right, yes,' said Chris. 'You know that Gerry found evidence Lyell had been watching killing sprees and mass murders on the dark web... She's gone through the hard drive in Lyell's laptop, and she found several more. Then she took a look at the memory stick you took from Lyell's pocket last night. I've got a copy on my iPad.' At a nod from Greg, she connected her iPad to the office wi-fi and projected her recording onto the screen at the end of the room.

At that magnification the images were fuzzy, and the wi-fi – as ever – struggled with video content and paused a couple of times to buffer. Even so, they watched in silence as the sleek woman in black leaned into the screen and with an icy composure informed them that she planned to die and take as many useless, self-obsessed and over-entitled feeble manifestations of manhood with her as possible. 'The gene pool can only benefit from preventing Brett Wallace and his like from breeding,' she said. 'I should have done this years ago.'

There was a silence in the room, which it seemed no one wanted to break. Eventually Greg said, 'I suppose her argument has a coherence of a kind, if you ignore the gap between fantasy and reality!'

'And you overlook the fact that she's stark staring barking,' interpolated Chris.

Greg took no notice. 'But it doesn't explain why she was so resentful,' he said. 'Lots of people get dumped. Thank God few of them decide to shoot up Norwich Railway Station as a result.'

There was another pause, then Greg added, 'I suppose we should distinguish between the questions we *need a*nswers to, and those we'd *like* answers to.'

'Where the cyanide crystals came from falls into the first category,' said Jim.

'Yes. And why she reacted to rejection the way she did, comes into the second. But I'd still like to understand,' said Greg.

Emerging from the meeting with at least some clarity about the questions, and the beginnings of a strategy to find the answers, Greg was surprised to find there was still silence from the superior denizens of the upper floor. Shaking his head in surprise, he was just about to pay another visit to Gerry the forensic expert when Chris came galloping into his office in her usual understated way. Catching the door on its return swing after the ricochet off the wall, Greg asked mildly, 'Something pressing, Chris?'

'I'll say,' she said. 'I've just heard from, well, shall we just say my usual sources on the top floor. The dingbat from the Met...' Greg had no trouble identifying DC Jeff Fellowes from this epithet, recent import from the Metropolitan Police and frequent recipient of Chris's ire. 'Word is, he's accused the Chief Super of being our mole. You know, the one we were supposed to be looking for until a certain train passenger imbibed cyanide from his homicidal ex and distracted us.'

'He's meant to be on suspension for distributing those inappropriate pictures of Sarah,' said Greg. 'How's he got involved with our investigation?'

'He hasn't. Not exactly. It seems that in the middle of his disciplinary interview about the photos of Sarah he put on WhatsApp, he suddenly declared that he'd trade info on our mole for a get-out-of-jail-free card.'

'They surely didn't fall for that?' exclaimed Greg.

'Not exactly. But when they expressed scepticism, he apparently said that if they cared to take a look at the offspring of a certain chief superintendent, they might find it worthwhile to explore where a substantial part of their income was coming from. And, moreover, why that same chief super was protecting the source of the income. Now the whole top floor is running round like headless poultry. Except for the Chief Constable, who is closeted with said Chief Super, and his secretary, who is looking for you.'

'For me!' exclaimed Greg. 'Why didn't you say so?'

'I just did,' said Chris. 'I just put it into context, that's all.'

Greg was looking round for his phone. It was, as usual when he couldn't find it, blamelessly on charge on the windowsill. Snatching it up, he headed for the door.

'I'd better go upstairs and see what they want. Can you chase down Gerry and check whether she's found anything else in Lyell's internet history?'

'Will do,' said Chris. 'And I've got a name in Defra of an old friend of hers. I'm going to see what else I can find out about her background. I'll take Bill with me. He can mooch around the office and see what else he can pick up.'

***

The open-plan Defra office space was, like many other such government offices, cramped and cluttered. According to the signs on the walls, desks were meant to be used by anyone rather than allocated to individuals. Judging by the amount of semi-domestic clutter on most desks and the personalised seating arrangements, this was a policy more honoured in the breach than the observance. While Bill 'mooched' as per instructions, chatting to anyone and everyone, Chris collected her official interviewee and headed for the conference room.

'I gather you've known Frances Lyell for a long time,' said Chris, the formalities out of the way.

'Since we were both in our twenties,' said the pale woman with hair in a straggly ponytail and broken veins on her cheeks signalling an outdoor life.

'But I thought Ms Lyell only transferred to Norwich relatively recently?'

'That's right. But I knew her in London before that.'

'I appreciate this must have been a shock to you, Sylvia,' said Chris, seeing the woman's hands shake as she picked up her glass of water and took a careful sip.

'It has,' she said. 'Fran was always very...' she hesitated, 'very black and white in her dealings with people. But I'd never imagined anything like this.' She looked for a moment as though she was going to be sick, took a deep breath and put her glass down carefully.

'What do you mean by "very black and white"?' asked Chris.

'Well, she was always either for you or against you, especially men. When she had a date, on the rare occasions she went out with someone, they were always the best thing ever for a few days. Then when they let her down, which they always did, they were absolute sh— ' She cut herself short. 'You know what I mean,' she added.

'You said she didn't often have dates,' said Chris. 'Why was that?'

'That was more recently. When we were both younger, she had lots of dates. She was very attractive, and they were like flies round a honeypot. I was a bit jealous, to be honest. But nothing ever lasted, and after a while she got a reputation for being a bit scary. I think she had two problems,' said Sylvia. 'First, her expectations were unrealistic. No man's perfect after all. Are they?' she appealed to Chris's shared experience as a woman. 'I think "shopping" for a man is a bit like buying a house. You need a few must-haves and plenty of would-like-to-haves, and you accept you won't get all the would-like-to-haves. For example, my must-haves include kindness, honesty and loyalty. I'm not so fussed about whether they're dark or fair, tall or short, or what they do for a living. Fran, on the other hand, she had nothing but a long list of must-haves and when they fell short, as inevitably they did, she dumped them like lightning. After a while, no one wanted to take the risk.'

'How did she react?' asked Chris.

'She got quite bitter. She started to say that all men were the same. Just like her father. But, on the other hand, she did want a relationship, which is why she tried online dating. To find a new pool to fish in.'

'What was it about her father?' asked Chris, jumping on the new factor.

'He left their home when she was twelve. Just walked out on her and her mother, and she never saw him again.'

'That's interesting,' said Chris. 'She told us he had died. Is he still alive?'

'No idea. Never met him. But he definitely walked out. I've never met her mother, come to that. She moved to Spain at least ten years ago. The father was off the scene long before I met Fran. I only know about him because of the remarks she passed, every time something went wrong with yet another relationship.'

'How did she get on in the office?' asked Chris. 'Were her work relationships difficult as well?'

'She got on pretty well with most people, except for those she dated and fell out with. At least one man asked for a transfer because of the atmosphere after they broke up. Luckily, frequent transfers are a fact of life in the civil service. We rarely stay anywhere more than four years, so mostly people could transfer out without it being a big deal.'

'On a rather different subject,' said Chris, 'it seems Frances Lyell had access to a couple of rather old agricultural pesticides. Do you have any idea where they might have come from?'

Sylvia hesitated for a moment. 'We all visit farms from time to time,' she said, 'and some old farmers do have a habit of holding on to old chemicals. It's the sort of stuff you used to find occasionally in the back of their pesticide stores. But I don't know of any specific examples, and it happens less and less these days. The whole sector is more professional than it used to be. What I will say is that Fran always maintained that you can get anything on the internet.'

Back in the car, the results of Bill's mooch around the office bore out what Sylvia had said to Chris.

'High IQ but not very good with people,' he summed it up, 'especially men and especially any she dated. The chaps I talked to said they'd been warned to steer clear. Too difficult, too demanding, and very spiteful after relationships broke down.'

'Anybody say anything about her family?' asked Chris.

'Only that she didn't have any. Mother in Spain and no mention of the father or any siblings. Sounds a lonely existence,' added Bill.

'Back to the office then, and let's hope Gerry's had more luck in her internet searches.'

***

Greg was watching a video clip on Gerry's laptop when they entered his office. He looked up as they came in.

'Anything new?' he asked.

'Not much. Just that Lyell had very high expectations of men and became very bitter and resentful when she was disappointed. Some suggestion that her attitude may have been connected with her father walking out when she was twelve. Nothing firm on access to chemicals. You?'

'Gerry's just showing me. In addition to the dark-web videos of mass killings, she's turned up a website where you can buy drugs to commit suicide with. It seems that's where she got the strychnine and the potassium cyanide. Nothing on the Cymag gassing powder.'

'No. Well, it's been suggested she may have picked that up out of an old farm chemical store, but we'll probably struggle to prove it. I checked the can on our way back up here. It has a label from an agricultural supply merchant, but they ceased trading a few years ago, so that's not going to help much.'

'I've passed what we have so far to the coroner, and I've run it past our legal team. The general view is that we'd have a good case against her on a charge of murder, if she were still alive, and that the evidence we've handed over from the shootings at the railway station is probably sufficient for the coroner to address the question of lawful or unlawful killing.'

'What about the inquests on the victims of her shooting spree?' asked Chris.

'Depends what questions the coroner comes up with. We've both made our reports of what happened leading up to our calling at her house that evening, and what happened since. The legal view is that those, together with the statements from Jim Henning plus Jones and his men, set out clearly the chain of events. We'll almost certainly be called to give evidence to the inquests, and they're bound to focus on why we didn't take precautions to prevent her making a run for it. With twenty-twenty hindsight, of course we should have done. But we had no reason, at the time, to think she posed that sort of threat. Anyway, there's nothing more we can do now, so unless the pre-inquest hearing on Lyell comes up with other questions, we're free to go back to work on the internal investigation.'

'But who do we report to now, if the Chief Super is in the frame?' asked Chris.

'He-Who-Must-Be-Obeyed,' replied Greg, using the station slang for the Chief Constable. 'That's where I was most of the morning. Bringing him up to speed and being told to get a move on before he gets his round objects nailed to the wall by the Home Secretary. I paraphrase,' he added. 'But let's get going before I find my round objects treated in like manner.'

THE END

About the Author

Award-winning author Heather Peck has enjoyed a varied life. She has been both farmer and agricultural policy adviser, volunteer covid vaccinator and NHS Trust Chair. She bred sheep and alpacas, reared calves, broke ploughs, represented the UK in international negotiations, specialised in emergency response from Chernobyl to bird flu, managed controls over pesticides and GM crops, saw legislation through Parliament and got paid to eat Kit Kats while on secondment to Nestle Rowntree.

She lives in Norfolk with her partner Gary, two dogs, two cats, two hens and a female rabbit named Hero.

Acknowledgments

My thanks to Sharon Gray at CluedUpEditing for her meticulous proof reading
and to my readers for their enthusiastic reception of the chapters serialised in my Newsletter.

If you would like to join their number by subscribing to my free newsletter you will find it at
www.heatherpeckauthor.com

Also by Heather Peck

THE DCI GELDARD NORFOLK MYSTERIES

Secret Places

Glass Arrows *

Fires of Hate **

The Temenos Remains **

Dig Two Graves **

Beyond Closed Doors

coming soon: Buried in the Past – DCI Geldard No 7

Death on the Rhine (novella)

Milestones (thriller)

BOOKS FOR CHILDREN

Tails of Two Spaniels **

The Pixie and the Bear

The Animals of White Cows Farm

*shortlisted for the East Anglian Book Award prize for fiction 2021

**Firebird Book Award Winner

Printed in Dunstable, United Kingdom

63411211R20068